Cage (Allen Securities #5)

by

Madison Stevens

Cage spent most of his life as a carefree bachelor. It was a good life with no attachments and a solid job working with his brothers to catch bad guys. Everything changed in an instant when he was crippled on the job, and he watched a man die to save his life.

Now, months later, Cage is still confronting the demons of self-worth and his guilt over the other man's death, along with growing feelings for Whitney, an attractive vet who seems to think he's still a shallow playboy.

Whitney doesn't want to get tangled up with a playboy. She thinks she knows Cage's type and would rather be alone than risk her heart getting torn apart.

When someone starts leaving strange items at her vet clinic, she finds the only man she can trust to help is the one man she's afraid of getting to know.

The two are forced to confront their feelings as they race to figure out why Whitney is being targeted.

Copyright © 2015 Madison Stevens

ISBN-13: 978-1523839032

ISBN-10: 1523839031

Cover designed by Najla Qamber Designs

CHAPTER ONE

CAGE MADE HIS WAY through the quiet graveyard. The damp grass squished beneath his boots with each step. The recent spring rain only served to make the whole trip that much more uncomfortable.

He stopped at a plain grave standing in the back of the cemetery. The headstone stood near a gravel road, which offered the potential for more traffic. Despite that, Cage doubted the place saw many visitors.

The brief weather respite gave way to more drops falling from the darkened sky. Rain slipped down the gray stone and wove its way along the letters engraved there: CARLOS FLORES.

The flowers in Cage's hand seemed heavy as he stared at the name. It had been nearly two months since the woods and the incident, and yet it was as fresh in his mind as if it happened just moments ago. A simple damn job that went south.

All they had to do was stop the idiots from setting the mountain on fire. That was it. The task had seemed like such an easy thing to pull off compared to a lot of jobs they'd had in the past. Cage and Reed were supposed to just go in and knock a few heads together. Just another day at the office. Nothing they hadn't done before. Maybe not on a mountain, but same basic job.

But Carlos had called and insisted on coming. They knew having him tag along was beyond a bad idea, but they had given in to the older man. After all, they all understood his position. He was fighting for his life.

He had to regain control of the Los Malos, or his days were numbered in the gang. Old ex-leaders didn't tend to last long. If you got booted from your position, you were weak. And gangs didn't need the weak, especially weak old men who didn't like the gang's plans.

So the old man came along.

Cage tightened his free hand into a fist as the details replayed themselves in his mind.

The whole thing had gone well at first. Being a thug wasn't the same thing as having discipline, especially discipline under fire. Most of the Los Malos weren't all that great with a gun. In the firefight, they were so worried about getting hit, they barely fired, and the few that did kept spraying bullets so wide Cage thought they'd been lucky to hit a freaking bus. Most of the tough guys fled on their bikes within the first ten minutes, despite outnumbering Reed, Cage and Carlos.

There had been only two left. Carlos had said they were the craftier ones. Actually tough. He had been right.

The two men had the advantage with the high ground and knew how to use it. They kept laying down fire, barely visible. No matter how good a shot Cage or Reed might have been, they needed a damn target to hit. The bikers, as if sensing the frustration, poured down even more bullets in a frenzy.

A few of the fleeing bikers found their balls and came back. So they ended up with four guys having the freaking high ground.

Then everything went wrong. Too damn wrong.

A wild bullet ripped through his knee. Still filled with adrenaline, Cage nailed the one that hit him in the upper left arm. The bastard deserved more than the flesh wound that he got, but the pain in his knee turned Cage's aim to shit. After his shot, he dropped to the ground, unable to stand, trying to gut-check his way through agony.

It was a split second. Not even enough time for him to think about it. A second shot rang through the air. Carlos turned as a bullet pierced his back.

Everything stilled around Cage as the old biker fell. In that moment, Cage recognized the truth. Carlos knew the shot was coming and stepped in front. He could've left Cage. Could've ran. The bikers would have taken the easy kill, the guy on the ground with a bullet in his knee.

Instead, Carlos took the bullet, the second bullet meant for Cage.

Cage squeezed off a quick shot, despite his pain, wounding another of the bikers. Reed took the opportunity to take out two more. The last guy jumped down, maybe hoping to get a final kill off of Cage, but Reed put a bullet in him.

Cage could still see the look on the old man's face as he fell to the ground. The look still haunted him at night.

He squeezed the flower stems and took in several deep breaths. This wasn't about the look on Carlos's face. Cage was going to have to put it out of his mind if he hoped to make it through this.

Today was about paying respects. Something he hadn't been able to do since they got back. He'd missed the funeral and had only been able to send flowers. It wasn't what he wanted. It wasn't what Carlos was owed for his sacrifice.

Cage loosened the grip he had on the flowers and leaned forward to place them against the grave.

His leg shook a little as he placed too much weight on it.

"Shit," he grunted and caught himself by grabbing the headstone.

Sweat beaded against his head, and he breathed in hard. His damn knee wasn't healing like he expected, but there was no helping it as the whole joint had been shattered. The doctor told him he was lucky to still be able to walk.

He looked down at his hand gripping the cold stone and let out a harsh laugh. The doctor was likely right, all things considered.

"Gotta save me again." He gave a sad smile. "I always

knew you were a show-off."

The smile slid from his face as he pushed himself back to standing and sighed.

Cage turned his face toward the sky. The earlier drizzle had given way to fat drops, but he stood like that for a moment, letting the cold water hit his face and take the sting from the day away.

After a moment he turned back to the stone and nodded. It might not mean much, but he wouldn't let the old man's death be for nothing. Cage would make a life enough for two people. He owed it to Carlos.

When he turned to head back to the car, his knee pulsed.

"Fucking rain," he muttered and gritted past the pain.

The car wasn't far away. He could make it.

Slowly, he made his way back and gripped the passenger door tightly. Getting things open and getting around had become a constant struggle.

"Should've brought the cane like I said," Trent said when he opened the door from the inside, his blue eyes filled with reproach.

Harley barked once from the backseat and then settled down. Nothing like a three-legged mastiff to take your mind off things.

Still sporting his post-military cut, the blond-haired Trent looked more like he was ready to head out on another SEAL mission rather than waiting on Cage's sorry ass to hobble back to the car.

Cage ignored the comment. He was getting good at that. Everyone was just trying to help, but he'd never build strength in his knee if he was always relying on something to help him walk. He didn't need that shit. He'd fight his way back.

"You can take the man out of the military, but you can't take the boss out of the man," Cage said, grinning at the longtime family friend.

Trent started the car and shook his head.

"What can I say? Some of us were just born to boss people around."

They wound their way through the cemetery. The rain beat quietly against the windows as the grave slowly disappeared in the mirror.

"You okay?" Trent asked quietly.

Everyone had been so good about avoiding the topic and giving Cage his space, except Trent. He'd only been out of the military for a few weeks but seemed to understand the situation from the start. Cage had to think it was from all the times that he'd seen friends sent home in a coffin.

Or maybe it was because of Trent's own experience. He'd been hit by a sniper. The shot tore through the side of his knee. Unlike Cage, his recovery had been better. Still hadn't made much difference with the SEALs, but it was understandable. They couldn't have him seizing up on a mission against some terrorists.

He looked over at the older man. As much as Cage had been through, Trent had been through worse, including losing his brother while he was still in school.

"I'm fine," Cage said. Talking about what had happened wasn't going to change anything. He just needed to move on. "When's the parole hearing?"

Trent's hands tightened on the steering wheel.

"Three weeks," Trent said. All the playfulness from earlier vanished.

Nearly ten years had passed since Trent's brother, Paul, had been murdered trying to save a teen girl from being raped. After all those years, it was the first time the bastard was up for parole. Trent planned on making sure that didn't happen. With the recent upswing in crime, no one was feeling all that confident about how things would turn out.

"We'll make sure that doesn't happen," Cage said.

Trent nodded and stayed quiet, but Cage knew better. The

gravity of the situation was not lost on any of them. It didn't help that Trent's sister and father were still in the area. No one thought any of them would be able to handle it if Paul's killer were allowed to roam free.

Cage sighed. They had all been through so much over the years. He could just hope that they all found some sort of peace.

He thought about his own brothers. In the last year, a lot of them had found happiness. Cage's mind drifted to the pretty vet he'd be seeing later. Not that he had a chance with her. Even before he'd been shot, Whitney wanted nothing to do with him. He didn't really expect things to have changed with her despite how much he had changed.

How could she know all that?

Two months down because of his knee. He looked down at his throbbing leg and tried not to picture the nasty scars that coated his knee. She wouldn't see all that with his pants covering it. All she would see was his walk.

Cage clenched his fist. He was more than his stupid knee.

Harley leaned over the seat and placed his head on Cage's shoulder as if he could sense his pain.

The sweet dog licked the side of Cage's face. He smiled.

Everything would go fine. He would go to the vet appointment and show Whitney the man he was. He'd prove to her that she should be with him and that he was worth it.

No big deal.

CHAPTER TWO

WHITNEY PULLED HER LAB COAT a little tighter and rubbed her hands together. The crisp, chilly air nipped at her. The temperature was a bit colder than it had been. It seemed like spring was taking longer to arrive. After the long winter, she was just about done with all the cold weather. It was enough to make her want to move to some place warm. Maybe Arizona.

She stopped at a cage where a little beagle lay. She had only found him this morning. The poor thing had been sprawled out on the back steps of the office. She could only guess that the person who hit him had placed him there. No one in the neighborhood seemed to know the little guy, and she was sure he was a runaway.

The cage squeaked a little as she pinched the locks together and opened the door. His tail thumped against the towel he was lying on, and she couldn't help but smile. The poor little guy had been through hell but still wanted someone to pet him. The resilience of animals always amazed her.

"Hey, Hank," she said and scratched the dog behind his ear.

He was lucky really. A dog that size usually didn't stand a chance against a car. Her best guess was that the car just clipped him. He had no broken bones, only some swelling and bruising around some ribs.

Mostly, though, he was fatigued. The pads on his feet were cracked and bleeding. He was coated in a layer of filth and grime. She needed to get him cleaned up, but there hadn't been time yet.

He also had a few major cuts on him, which she assumed were from other animals. She had checked for a chip but found nothing.

Whitney stroked his soft ears and sighed as her auburn hair slipped in front of her face. The pup was going to live, but she couldn't keep doing this. If she took in every stray, she was going to be the crazy old lady living by herself with her zoo.

Hank nuzzled her hand and swiped his warm puppy tongue across her palm.

"You don't fight fair."

His tail thumped the towel a few more times, and she sighed. She was totally getting a new puppy.

"Any news on him?" Lisa said as she came from around the corner.

Whitney shook her head.

"I just can't figure it out," she said and pulled her hand back. The cage rattled a little as she closed it, but the dog didn't seem to mind.

"I know," Lisa said and whipped off the gloves she was wearing. Her long brown hair swung against her back as she did so. "You'd think fur parents would know better."

Whitney shook her head.

"It's not that," she said and glanced back to the sleeping puppy. "I'm just sure he's not a street dog. He just doesn't have that feel."

Lisa snorted. "What? Is he missing the tattoos that give him his cred?"

Whitney grinned back. She knew hiring the vet tech from where she volunteered would be a great idea. They had been working for years together, and Whitney knew Lisa was more than capable. Not only that, she needed the help. Things were picking up, and Whitney needed to count on someone else besides Sharon, her cranky but efficient receptionist.

"He's young," Whitney said. "And he just seems soft."

Lisa raised an eyebrow. "You know you spend too much time around animals, don't you?"

Whitney huffed and walked to the fridge around the corner to grab her water bottle. "It's my job. Of course I do. What would you have me do?"

She took a drink from the water bottle and slammed the fridge shut.

"Get laid," Lisa said with a shrug.

The water slipped down the wrong way, and Whitney coughed, trying to take in a breath.

"What?" she finally said after managing to avoid drowning while standing.

Lisa handed her a paper towel and sighed. "When was the last time you had a date?"

Whitney wiped off her mouth and scowled at Lisa. "What do you mean? I went for coffee with Ted just the other day after we finished our rotation."

This time it was Lisa's turn to frown, after a little eye roll.

"I mean with a man you are actually interested in," Lisa said and paused for a moment. "Interested in sexually, that is."

Whitney started to open her mouth to protest but snapped it shut.

She liked Ted. She really did. He was nice and polite. They had tons to talk about since they were both veterinarians, but sexually? Not a thing. Not even a little zing. Whitney had thought that if she got to know him, maybe there would be something, but it was almost the opposite.

The more she knew him, the less interested she was in being with him. There was no chemistry, no hint of sparks.

"I just don't understand," Lisa said, following Whitney out of the little break room and back into a large room in the back of the clinic. "If you aren't interested in him like that, why do you keep seeing him? You're just wasting both your time and his. Even if he's not hot to get into your pants immediately, he's going to eventually want a physical relationship."

Whitney stopped over by a cage to look at the cat inside. She picked up the clipboard and checked all the recent vitals.

Trying to explain to others why she acted the way she did was nearly impossible. What was she supposed to tell them? That her dad, who she loved dearly, liked to run around on her mother? That he and her mother had been so in love with love they hadn't thought about the long-term implications?

She shook her head. There was no way she could say that. Some things other people just didn't need to know.

"Ted is a solid man," Whitney said firmly and turned to look at Lisa. "I just need a little companionship. Not everything is about sex."

Lisa shook her long hair and crossed her arms. "You aren't doing either of you any favors. Trust me. End it soon before anyone gets too invested the wrong way with the wrong expectations."

Whitney winced. Lisa was right. It wasn't like the thought hadn't crossed her mind. She was just looking for a good chat, but Ted was looking for a wife.

Her shoulders slumped forward, and she nodded.

"I know," she said and looked down. "I'm just tired of being alone."

The front door dinged, and Lisa went to the glass to peek out.

"There's someone to not be alone with," Lisa said with a grin.

Whitney stood on her tippy toes to look through.

"Shit," she breathed out.

What the hell was Cage Allen doing there? It wasn't supposed to be him standing there at the counter looking like some sort of brown-haired sex god. She licked her lips.

Had she really just thought of him as a sex god? Lord

help her, that was about all she could think of him as. His fit body seemed to strain against his t-shirt.

A sour taste attacked her mouth. He was more a sex expert than a sex god, and that was really just from experience. Even his sister had said that Cage slept around a lot. That was really no surprise though. With his looks, he could pretty much have who he wanted. Maybe Whitney was wrong to only want Ted to chat with, but Cage just wanted someone to warm his bed for a few nights.

She stepped back from the door and straightened herself.

"You take him," Whitney said.

Lisa dragged her eyes away from the door to look at her. "What?"

Whitney moved back to the cat chart she was looking at. "It's fine. Harley is just in for a check-up. Get me if you notice anything."

Lisa sighed and shook her head.

"You know," Lisa said, her eyes narrowed, "sometimes I think you're a coward."

* * *

Cage waited inside a little room with a table and prayed that no one was going to ask him to lug that big dog up on the table. He stared at the mastiff, who was resting his head on Cage's sore knee.

He wanted to laugh. Even the damn dog seemed to want to protect him from getting hurt.

Maybe Harley understood what he was going through. Cage looked over the dog's remaining three legs. Harley knew what it was like to be hurt trying to take down bad guys.

"I'm fine," he said to Harley.

Harley's black ears twitched a little, and he snorted in reply.

Cage pressed his lips together. "You sound like Meg."

Harley's ears perked up at the mention of his human mother, and Cage couldn't help but smile. Having a conversation with a dog might make him crazy, but at least he could win that one.

A few short raps came from the door.

Despite himself, his palms started to sweat. He didn't want Whitney to see him this way. Well, that wasn't totally true. He had fought with his sister to even take Harley in, but he didn't want the pretty red head to think he was weak.

His knee didn't define him. Cage was far from weak, and he'd do what he needed to in order to prove that.

Of course, to prove anything, he'd need to convince her to give him the time of day. The last time he'd tried, she totally shot him down. That wasn't exactly something he was used to. Then he went and got his knee blown out by a bullet, and he couldn't even attempt to talk to her for a long time.

A taller woman with long brown hair stepped in, and he suppressed the frown that tried to come up.

"Cage?" The woman said and stuck out her hand. "I'm Lisa. Doctor Carter asked me to check on Harley while she deals with another patient."

He forced down his frustration. It wasn't like he could be mad at a veterinarian for saving some other animal's life. After the amazing job she did with Harley when he had been shot, he could only imagine that she was in high demand.

"Thanks," he said and took her hand without standing.

Luckily, Harley seemed to take over, knowing that he was the star of the show.

"And you must be Harley."

Lisa squatted down and grinned at the large dog.

Harley panted at her as she scratched his head with her nails.

"How is he doing?" Lisa asked.

Cage gave the big dog a pat. "Good. Meg said he's getting around great. No issues with the stairs now."

"Good boy," she said and laughed when the dog stood a little taller.

There was something about her that seemed familiar. He just couldn't place it. Sweat beaded on his brow as he tried to think. Lord help him if he'd slept with her. His only hope was that he'd remember before she did. Otherwise, his chances with Whitney were shot.

"How's the wound looking?" Lisa asked and touched the scar where Harley's left front leg used to be.

Harley leaned hard on him, and Cage grunted as the large dog shifted his weight to press hard against his damaged knee. He knew the feeling. The tissue there was still very sensitive.

"It's looking great," she said and pulled back her hand. She spent a few long moments checking his vitals.

Lisa smiled at Harley and stood.

"That's it," she said to him. "I think we're good to wait another six months."

He nodded and stood, doing his best to keep any sign of pain out of his face. The strain on his knee was killing him, but he could make it.

Lisa walked to the door and stopped. When she turned, her face paled a little.

"Cage Allen?" she said. "Of course. I don't know why I didn't make the connection between Meg Allen and you from the chart."

Here it came. The moment of truth. Cage opened his mouth to respond but instead nodded, unsure of what to even say.

"Oh. You're probably confused." She held up a hand. "I know your brother Kace. Well, kind of know."

She shook her head as if she were shaking out some bad memory. He could only hope that she knew Kace in a personal and not professional way. Kace might have left the cop life behind, but he had been a police officer for a long time, and there were all sorts of unfortunate ways she might have run into him when he was wearing the blue.

"It's been years though," she said with a smile. "Small world."

Cage nodded. Whatever had happened between her and Kace was years ago. Maybe they'd briefly dated in high school or something. It wasn't like Cage had carefully paid attention to every girl his brothers went out with years earlier.

"He's married with a kid on the way," he said, somewhat testing the water.

She smiled warmly. "That's great. I'm glad to hear it."

Cage nodded. "Should I tell him hi from you?"

Lisa shook her head. "Best not to." She smiled and patted Harley on the head. "You be a good boy, handsome."

Cage watched as she hurried off and wondered what the hell that was all about. Slowly, he made his way to the front with Harley and stopped at the counter. The nasty receptionist glared at him. He'd hadn't been in for two months, but she apparently hadn't forgotten him either.

"I'll just have Meg schedule the appointment," he said to her.

The plump older woman scowled at him. "That would be best," she snapped.

He ignored her and made his way outside, where Trent was waiting in the car.

"Well?" Trent said as Harley took his place in the back seat.

"No go," he said. "She didn't come."

"Why don't you just show up and ask her out?" Trent asked.

Cage looked back to the office.

"Maybe," he said and sighed. "I think first thing we need to drop off this guy if we plan on going out tonight." He looked over to Trent, somewhat hoping he'd changed his mind. "Are we going out?"

"Oh, don't even try to get out of this." Trent grinned and shifted the car into gear. "Your ass is getting out of the house."

Cage looked out the window as the office disappeared from sight.

"I thought I was out of the house," he grumbled.

CHAPTER THREE

SEVERAL MEN GROANED as the large dog entered the security firm's building, but Cage didn't give a shit. They could all go to hell as far as he was concerned. The dog saved his sister, and that was more than he could say for some of them. If anyone had something to say about it, they could say it to him first.

"Somebody hide the doughnuts," Kace shouted up the stairs. "Meg's beast is here."

Harley tilted his head at the mention of doughnuts and looked around for his favorite treat. Cage sighed. It wasn't like the big dog could help it if idiots left something yummy out where he could get to it. If they wanted to eat the damn things, they should have thought about it.

"Oh," Meg said from the top of the stairs. "Is Kace being a dick to my little man?"

Harley pulled a little on his leash and thumped his tail hard against the floor, just like every time he saw her.

Cage let go of the leash before the dog pulled him over.

Meg stooped to meet him as he bolted up the stairs, moving without much trouble, despite his three-leg handicap

"How was the appointment?" she asked. Her longer hair made her look a little sweeter than normal, but he could sense the venom behind her words.

"She was busy," he said and turned away. It wasn't like he wanted to be given the third degree by everyone.

Meg stared at him for a moment before going on.

"So what did they say?"

Cage turned back to her. Worry clouded her expression.

"He's doing great," he said with a smile. "They said they don't need to see him for six months."

Meg nodded and pulled the dog closer. The whole ordeal had taken a bit more out of her than she liked to let on, but he knew the truth. She was his sister after all.

"Good," she said and stood. Harley popped up next to her. "Thanks for taking him," she said. She started to turn but stopped. A grin split her face. "And thanks for not getting me dropped as a patient."

"What's that supposed to mean?"

She snorted. "Sexually harassing my vet would be a good way to get her to kick me to the curb."

Cage rolled his eyes. He knew he was going to have to deal with this from the others. They just didn't understand that he'd changed. Hell, half the time he didn't even understand it himself, but he couldn't keep going like he had been before the mountain and the death of Carlos.

Cage wanted more from life. Or more than he'd been getting. He needed something meaningful, not just sex with women he barely cared about.

He watched as Meg took the large dog upstairs and disappeared around the corner. Suddenly, the stairs seemed far more daunting than before. Trent brushed past him and quickly made it to the top.

"Show-off," Cage grumbled to himself.

Cage slowly climbed the stairs. He looked over at the rail and glared at it. He'd be damned if he used that thing like some old man.

"Don't be a dumbass," Reed said from the top of the stairs. "Use the fucking rail."

Cage glared up at his older brother. Reed might be the owner of the security firm, and his boss, but he'd be damned if he was going to let Reed tell him what to do.

He ignored the disapproving grunt and made his way up.

When he finally reached the top, Reed sighed and clapped him on the shoulder.

"You know, sometimes you can be a real idiot," Reed said.

"Try staying with him," Trent said from around the corner.

"Whatever," Cage said and glared at the two men. They might be well-meaning, but the last thing he needed was another lecture. It wasn't like his mother wasn't already on him to use the cane she bought.

It didn't help that the damn thing was shiny green and made him look like a pimp. All the men at the firm had a good laugh over it, and there was no way he'd be caught dead with that thing. "We doing this meeting or what?"

Reed nodded to the door down the hall.

"The others are already in there," he said to Cage and then turned to Trent. "Any word from Johnny?"

Trent nodded. Cage knew he was keeping in close contact with their childhood friend. He only had a few more months before he would be out of the Navy like Trent.

"They are giving him shit about wanting out," Trent said. "I've told him he doesn't have to leave because they don't want my sorry ass, but he's not hearing any of it."

Reed nodded as they walked down the hall.

"It's a big move," Reed said and ran a hand across his five-o'clock shadow.

Trent wrinkled his nose. "You're telling me."

They stopped outside the conference room.

"You could still go back," Reed said. "They would take you."

Trent shook his head. "Not as a SEAL, and what's the point if I'm not doing the job I was trained for?"

Cage could understand that. He had been feeling a little low since being shot. This was the only job he was good at. What the hell else would he do? It's not like he was good with computers like Meg.

"Well," Reed said, smiling at Trent. "We're damn happy to have an ex-SEAL."

"Yeah, well, now you just need to figure out where the hell I'm going," Trent said and grinned at him.

Cage frowned. "I thought Texas was a sure thing."

Reed shook his head. "Lot of things going on around here," he said. "I want to know what the hell is going on before I make a decision. With Finn and his men getting out of the black market business, things have gone all to shit. And with the Russian mafia and the Los Malos setting things on fire or blowing stuff up, we can't be certain what's going to happen."

Cage nodded. They really hadn't had a moment's rest recently. It seemed like their mostly quiet city had come alive, and, unfortunately, the recent action wasn't exactly being pushed by good people who cared about others.

"Let's get in," Reed said. "We've got a lot of shit to go over."

Cage groaned. He had a feeling this was not going to be a short meeting.

* * *

"You never mentioned he was an Allen boy," Lisa said as they fed the last dog. The CLOSED sign had already been turned over, and they were just about ready to go.

Whitney looked over at her friend from the computer, where she was logging the day's final notes.

"Who?" she asked.

Lisa crossed her arms and tossed her long brown hair over her shoulder. She raised a brow. "We going to play that game?"

Whitney snorted and went back to her computer screen.

"Fine," she said. "So his last name is Allen. You saw the chart. What's the problem?"

Lisa grabbed the broom from the wall and started to sweep.

"No problem," she said quickly. "Not just any Allen, though. Those Allens. I just didn't know. Their family is kinda known."

"In what way?" Whitney turned to look at her friend.

Lisa smiled and shook her head. "I'm surprised you didn't know, especially given what happened to Harley. The Allens sort of deal with things," she said and sighed in a dreamy way that made Whitney frown.

"What do they deal with?"

Lisa snapped out of her dazed state. "Oh, you know. Kidnappings, money laundering, shoot-outs. That kind of stuff."

Whitney sat up quickly and stared in shock at the lackadaisical way Lisa described the Allens. She acted like shootings were something common place.

"Why would they be involved with that sort of stuff?" Whitney said with a frown.

"They do security contracting." Lisa shrugged and put the broom back. The dustpan slipped off the wall. "Maybe because of those mob guys they know. You know, the Kellys?"

"What?"

Whitney nearly choked on the words. No wonder their dog had been shot. The Allens were trouble with a capital T, and she wanted nothing to do with that.

"Look," Lisa said quietly, "they aren't bad people. They're the good guys, and he seemed really disappointed you weren't there."

"No," she said simply. Whitney shook her head. "He's the last type of person I want to get involved with."

Lisa knelt down to push the pile of dust into the pan. "What? Super-hot and sexy?"

Whitney pushed her red hair behind her ear and looked back at the computer screen.

"That's the problem." She sighed. "You know I just can't. I don't want that."

Lisa stared at her as she dumped out the pan and placed it on the wall.

"Just make sure you aren't cutting off every chance for happiness because you aren't certain," Lisa said solemnly. "Life is too short to spend playing it safe. You already aren't satisfied with the perfectly safe type of guy. Just ask Ted."

Whitney knew Lisa was right, but the situation just wasn't something she could deal with. Before she thought Cage was just a playboy, but now she suspected he was some sort of adrenaline junky as well.

Men like Cage didn't stay. They didn't want boring, safe vets as girlfriends, and she didn't want to have to pick up the pieces like her mother did. It didn't make him bad, but that didn't mean she wanted to take the risk, no matter how much she wondered what his abs looked like under his shirt.

"You about ready to get dressed?" Lisa said.

"What?" The stool Whitney was sitting teetered a little. She tried to right herself.

"Oh, I don't think so," Lisa said and crossed her arms over her chest. "You are so not getting out of this."

Whitney sighed. She really hadn't meant to put it completely out of her mind, but the idea of going dancing now seemed really bad.

"Come on," Lisa whined a little. "You've got to get out and have a little fun."

Whitney frowned. "I have fun."

Lisa raised a brow. "When?"

Whitney pressed her lips together as she thought. Was it really that hard for her to think of the last time?

"Oh," she nearly shouted. "Every Sunday."

Lisa snorted. "When we volunteer? I don't think that really counts."

Whitney frowned. "Why? I like volunteering."

"You are so hopeless." Lisa smiled, and Whitney felt a little better. "Come dance with me. It will be fun."

"I don't know."

"Look, if Ted's too safe, and Cage's too dangerous, then maybe you can find your perfect middle guy at a club."

Whitney looked at the time on her screen. Only six. They would have plenty of time.

"Fine, but don't expect me to dance well."

Lisa grinned at her. "After a few drinks, I'm pretty sure you'll dance just fine."

Whitney laughed. "We'll see I guess."

CHAPTER FOUR

CAGE SAT WITH TRENT, LIAM AND FINN at a table in the corner of the club, music thumping around them. It hadn't been on top of his list to go out, but they needed to meet with the brothers to talk about the mounting issues with Los Malos.

Liam's buzzed short hair made him seem far more severe than they knew him to be. At least the way he used to be. He had only recently found out about his mob family heritage and that the head of the Kelly Clan, Finn, was his brother. Perhaps Liam's short time with the Kelly Clan had hardened him more than any of his former co-workers realized. Then again, maybe not, given he was with Meg.

Cage suppressed a chuckle. He knew all too well how time could change a man.

"So this Roberto is in charge now?" Liam said, his mouth a firm line.

Trent nodded. "As far as we can tell. There hasn't been a lot of noise from them recently, but something's going on with them. They aren't rolling over just because a few guys got hurt and thrown in jail. If anything, they're probably more pissed off."

Finn rubbed a hand over his face and frowned, his green eyes filled with irritation Even if he was taking the Irish mafia out of their illegal ventures, that didn't mean he didn't hear things.

"I'm not hearing much these days. Charlie is the best contact we've got now," he said and looked over to Cage.

The help Charlie had offered Ryder during their issues

with the Los Malos and Blitz, the dangerous biker from the west, had only increased their contact with the pawn shop owner, who always seemed to have a hand in everything going on.

Olivia, Reed's wife, hadn't been too happy with the recent events but was glad that the help had saved her friends. Without it, several women wouldn't have gotten out of the situation alive.

"Ryder's been talking with him, and all he had to add was that there were a few more containers coming in," Cage said. He sighed. "He thinks that working with us is ruining his cred around town. He's getting pushed out."

Finn nodded. They all knew how easily things could shift if certain people thought they were no longer able to speak freely.

"Maybe I'll make a purchase there soon," Finn said and looked to Liam. "Might have some impact." He smirked at Cage. "Even if we're getting out of lot of the business, people know we're not the Allens' bitches."

Cage snorted but kept silent. He wasn't going to let Finn get under his skin so easily.

Liam shrugged. "Couldn't hurt."

Finn leaned back and placed his hands behind his head.

"So what's the deal?" He nodded to Trent. "You the replacement for my brother?"

Trent shrugged. "Seems like you've got a lot going on around here."

They had been over this so many times Cage was tired of talking about it. He knew what was going on. With Liam working with Finn, and Cage's knee still messed up, they were down two men. Reed was just trying to make sure they were covered, especially with how unstable the city had been in the past months.

Cage turned away from the men and scanned the floor. They had started to come to this club more and more. If anything, they did it just because they knew there was safety in numbers. The Kellys and the Allens had plenty of enemies, after all.

His gaze stopped on deep red hair that bobbed in the crowd.

"You've got to be kidding me," he said. He clenched his teeth as he watched the pretty redhead move in a steady rhythm against some man. The man's hands dipped lower and lower toward her ass.

Cage stood, his chair scraping against the floor.

"What the…" Trent started but stopped when he followed Cage's line of sight. "Fuck."

Cage looked back to the men. "I've got shit to deal with," he said firmly and strolled over to the dance floor, doing his best to ignore his knee.

The beat thumped through her body as Whitney bounced around. The two shots she'd done had gone right to her head, but at this point, she didn't really care much. Actually, at this moment, she was trying to figure out how to escape Mr. Grabby Hands without just bolting away.

She jumped when firm hands pulled her into a wall of flesh.

"How about a glass of water?"

With the room somewhat spinning, she looked up into warm brown eyes.

"Cage?" she breathed out. "I… What?"

He pulled on her hand a little. "Water."

The other man found her other hand, and she pulled back from Cage a little.

"I'm dancing," she said and turned back to the other man, who grinned at her. She swallowed down the annoyance she was feeling. This wasn't exactly the situation she wanted to end up in.

She jumped when Cage's warm body slid behind her. The

other man frowned.

"Yo," the man said and stepped forward, squishing her further against Cage. "You heard her. We're dancing, bro."

"Yeah," Cage said behind her. She could feel his muscles tense and hoped it didn't break out into a fight, especially if she was between them. "And now she's with me."

The man glared at them both and then stormed off to the other side of the dance floor. Relief flooded Whitney as the man departed. She wasn't interested in wherever he wanted to take things.

"Let's get you a water," Cage rumbled from behind her.

Despite herself, Whitney could feel her temper rising. She wasn't one to be told what to do, even if Cage had helped her out.

"Just because that guy's gone doesn't change the fact that I'm dancing," she said and stepped away from him.

His hand slid around her middle, and she found herself pressed even harder against him.

"So dance," he said quietly in her ear.

She shivered as his breath brushed the hair on her neck, and she had to take in deep breaths to keep herself calm. Whitney tilted her head back a little to stare at him. The playful smile was on his face, and something in her wanted to wipe it off.

It was like he was taunting her, like she wasn't capable of being sexy. Well, she'd show him. After all, he was the one who was chasing her.

Whitney swayed her hips from side to side. Her short, black dress clung to her like a second skin, and she knew he'd be able to see down the low neckline as she moved, but for once, she didn't care. Maybe it was the shots talking, but she'd take the liquid courage all the same.

His hands gripped her hips, and she shivered when he groaned. One of his hands slid up her side, brushing the side of her breast as he continued along. She gasped when his rough fingers arrived at the tender flesh of her arm. She wound her arms around the back of his neck.

She threaded her fingers through his brown hair. His hair was softer than she had imagined. Her eyes closed as she ran her nails along his neck and listened to the rumble it caused.

She shut out the little voice in her head telling her that this was a very bad idea and just let the feeling of the music take over. One night. It couldn't hurt to trust for just one night. Maybe she was wrong. Maybe everything Lisa had said was right. There had to be more. She wanted there to be more. She couldn't let the shadow of her parents keep her from ever even really trying to find someone.

This time, when her hips moved, she pressed back into him. She could feel him. She'd have to be stupid not to feel him there. Hard and hot. Whitney could already feel her nipples straining against the tight black dress, desperate to be touched by those rough hands.

"Fuck," Cage said and tried to move back.

Whitney turned quickly in his arms and stared up at him.

"Look," Cage said, staring at her. She could hear the uncertainty in his voice. "I don't know what's going on—"

He stopped when she pushed in closer.

"Just do it," she said.

Cage stared at her. She could feel his soft eyes burning a hole into her. Her tongue darted out to wet her suddenly dry lips.

"Fuck it," he grunted and pressed her firmly against his hard body.

Softer than she would have thought, Cage pressed his mouth to hers. The loud music and the world around them faded. All she could hear was the thumping of her heart in her ears.

His hand slipped through her hair, and she sighed. Standing with him, being held by him, warmed her. He sparked something in her, and she felt the heat burn through her.

Whitney gasped when his rough hand wrapped around her just above her ass and pulled her closer into him. Her hands traced along his chest, and she reveled at the feel of his hard muscles under her fingers. Everything in her ached to slip under his shirt and feel the heat of those firm muscles.

She opened her mouth to him, and he pushed in with his tongue. Mint. All she could taste was mint, and it was so very him. Fresh.

Whitney pulled herself even closer and hitched a leg up against him.

Suddenly, there was air between them. Cage pulled back slightly.

His breathing was hard, and he shook a little as he spoke.

"Not like this," he said between breaths and placed his head against hers.

She nodded, not quite knowing what had happened, disappointment washing through her.

"Let's get that water," he said and opened his eyes.

She stared at him for a moment. Something about the way he stared at her made her feel as if she'd just been naked in front of him. Whitney took in a deep breath and looked down. Looking at him was harder than she thought. The way he looked at her made her feel more exposed than she was comfortable with. She thought he'd been the one chasing, that she had control, but in just a few short minutes the situation had been reversed.

She turned and hurried from the floor to a table where Lisa was sitting.

"I need to go," Whitney said.

Lisa frowned. "What's going on?"

Whitney glanced over her shoulder and didn't see Cage anywhere. She turned back to Lisa and leaned closer, so she'd be able to hear.

"He's here," she whispered.

Lisa leaned back and frowned. Her silver dress illuminated

her face as overhead light bounced off the shiny material.

"Who?" Lisa said.

Whitney frowned. Didn't anyone know what the hell was going on?

"Cage," she said.

As if she'd conjured him, Cage called to her from the corner of the room, at a table with several other handsome men, his voice nearly swallowed by the club music.

The women turned, and Whitney felt the butterflies in her stomach start up again. Those two shots weren't going to stay in her for long if this kept up.

Cage watched as Whitney glanced to the door and just hoped that she wouldn't run. He knew it was a bad idea to dance with her. Everything in him wanted to do more than dance, and that wasn't what he wanted from her.

Well, it was but not just that. She was different, and he wanted more. He wanted the chance to be with her.

The vet tech from earlier stood next to her, looking confused. He wondered what they'd been discussing.

To his relief, they made their way over to the table.

"That's the vet?" Trent said from the table.

Cage leaned heavily against the chair in front of him. Moving his knee like he had on the dance floor made it throb, but it had totally been worth it. Holding her in his arms had been all he could think about since first meeting her, when she had stood up for Harley to that bitchy front-desk woman. That short encounter had shown him all he needed to know. He knew that she was his kind of woman. He just needed to convince her of that.

His eyes locked with hers as she moved closer. Her cheeks were still flushed from the dance floor, and the red only seemed to spread the closer she got. Cage couldn't help but love the sweet look on her.

"You remember Lisa," she said quietly. She glanced over

to him and then to the other men at the table.

Cage nodded to Lisa and turned back to the men.

"Trent, Liam and Finn," he said and pointed to the men. They all offered her polite nods.

Cage grabbed a glass of water from the table and handed it to Whitney. "You should cool off."

Whitney took the glass and glanced back down.

"Fat chance," she mumbled.

His heart thumped loudly in his chest. Maybe he actually had a chance. He had to stop doubting himself and just go for it. Sometimes you just had to make the move.

"How about I take you home?" he said.

Her gaze shot to him, the pretty green eyes alluring, and Cage had to stamp down the desire that raced through him at the sight.

She opened her mouth to say something but stopped.

"Hey, baby," someone purred in his ear.

Cage turned just in time to watch as Sheryl slid up beside him, her large breasts on full display and pressed firmly against him.

"I was thinking you could take me to that place we like to go." She winked.

His stomach lurched at the timing.

"Well," Whitney snapped. He winced at the anger in the simple word. "Looks like you don't have time for that ride," she said. She shot him a burning look.

The other men at the table watched in silence, their expressions rather blank.

"No," he said quickly and tried to move away, but his damn knee wasn't cooperating. "It's not like that."

Whitney looked between them, and everything from earlier was gone.

"It's fine, Cage," she said stiffly and set the water down.

He watched as she walked away with her friend and felt the dull ache of rejection seep in.

"It's fine, baby," Sheryl whispered in his ear. "I'm here."

Cage clenched his fists. "And like I told you the last time you called, I don't want that. Not from you. Not anymore."

He moved stiffly to the closest chair and sank into it.

Cage looked up and found her glaring back at him.

"Whatever," she hissed. "It's not like I think your crippled ass would even be able to perform. I was just offering you a pity fuck."

She turned quickly on her high heels and stomped away.

Cage bit down the rage.

"Well," Finn said after they sat in silence a moment. "I think that went well."

CHAPTER FIVE

CAGE JUMPED at the sound of banging, trying to remember where he was.

Clarity returned, along with a piercing headache. He was at his place, in his own bed.

"Can't sleep all day," Trent said, banging on the door again.

Cage rolled over in his bed and groaned. Maybe all those shots last night weren't such a great idea. He knew it was a bad idea when Finn was the one leading the way. Finn might be leading the mob away from shadier shit, but that didn't make him any less a prick. He probably enjoyed seeing Cage flame out in the club.

Cage kept his eyes closed as he tried to block out the light from the window over his bed. Right then, he would have given anything if someone came along and gagged the bastard banging on his door.

The door hit the wall as Trent threw it open.

"No time to wallow in your pity party for one," he said.

The dresser squeaked as Trent pulled it open.

Cage opened an eye and tried to ignore the throbbing.

"Fuck off," he grumbled and rolled back over. The only thing he wanted to do was sleep off the massive hangover he had and try to forget about the two massive rejections he'd just suffered. It's not like he never got turned down, but two close together was much.

In truth, what Sheryl said shouldn't have bothered him, but it did. She was good at that sort of thing, picking out a person's weakness and playing on it. There he was, running over her words until he couldn't stand to think it anymore, even though he knew from his time on the dance floor with Whitney that he was more than ready to perform in bed.

Really though, he cared less about Sheryl and more about Whitney. Things had been going well. He felt the connection and knew she had as well. Now, she just thought he was the same old Cage and probably wouldn't give him the time of day.

"Get up," Trent said and slammed the drawer shut. "We've got some snooping to do."

Cage rolled back over and frowned. "Reed said I'm off."

Trent smirked at him. "Oh, I'm sorry," he said sarcastically. "I didn't realize you'd had your balls shot off as well. Nobody mentioned that to me."

Cage flipped him off and sat up.

"Besides," Trent said, walking over to the door. "When have you ever listened to your older brother?"

The door clicked shut behind him, and Cage shook his head. He had to admit that Trent certainly knew how to get a person going.

As quickly as he could manage despite his throbbing head, he got ready. It had been a while since he'd had an assignment, and it felt good knowing that he might be of help.

When he stepped into the living room, he was feeling much better. Although, with the smell of eggs in the air, he wasn't likely to last long.

"Breakfast is on the table," Trent said and nodded behind him.

Cage grabbed a piece of toast and choked it down. He figured something absorbing all that stuff in his stomach ought to help fight his nausea.

"What's the plan?" he asked and took a seat on the couch.

Odd as it might seem, he actually hated all his furniture now. Before, it had always been about comfort, but nothing was all that comfortable now, as it was all so low to the ground it was harder to get out of. Cage shifted a little and stretched out his sore leg.

"I say we do a little casing of the parts shop," Trent said and shoveled in a mouthful of eggs.

Cage looked away and swallowed.

"Isn't Reed on that?" he asked.

"He is, but mostly at night," Trent said. "I have a feeling this situation is different."

Cage shrugged and nodded. "Makes sense."

Trent set down his plate, and Cage looked over at him.

"After," Trent said, scrubbing a hand over his face, "I've made a call to my buddy."

Cage frowned. "The dog guy?"

Trent held up a hand. "Just hear me out."

Cage set down the toast and struggled to stand from the couch.

"No," he grunted as all his weight shifted to his leg. "I don't want that. I don't need that."

"Don't be a dumbass." Trent stood and offered a hand.

Cage glared at him and worked his way through the pain as he stood.

"I don't need help," he said and tried to back away.

"You do," Trent said and stepped right up to him. "Either way, I'm going to meet with Mark. If you choose to not talk to him, that's on you."

Cage glared at him and turned away. He was so fucking sick of having this same talk. Maybe if he just met the guy, everyone would back off.

"Fine," he said and made his way to the table. "But let's go, so I don't have to smell your shitty eggs anymore."

Trent frowned. "What's wrong with my eggs? I even added chives."

* * *

Whitney scrubbed the floor hard around the cages and grunted in frustration at the stain that just wouldn't seem to come up. Actually, she'd been frustrated since last night by the man that was to never be named in her presence again.

She moved her arms even faster against the stain and ignored the burn. Maybe she'd be able to work out her irritation by scrubbing the floor instead of finding the smooth-talking man and kicking him squarely between the legs, which is what she'd been fantasizing about and not other things that had to do with that area that she had clearly felt last night.

No. Nothing like that.

Leaning back, she gave her arms a break for a moment. She couldn't believe she fell for his game.

Part of her wondered if she should be thanking Cage. Without his playboy ways, there would be no way she'd have the energy to get all this cleaning done. As it stood now, she was looking at finishing ahead of time. Lemons and lemonades and all that.

Hank barked beside her and wagged his little tail. He'd been feeling much better, and she'd decided to let the little guy spend some time with her. She loved his resilience and was going to have a hard time giving him up when they found his owners. They were probably out there, looking for him at that very moment.

She scratched behind his ear and smiled.

"So uncomplicated," she whispered to the little dog. That was one of the reasons she loved animals so much.

The dog's head jerked to the door as something rustled outside.

Whitney looked at the door and thanked God that she'd thought to lock it. It wasn't like she was in the best neighborhood. Some junkie might think he could score something fun.

She slowly moved across the room and peeked out the window shade. The bright sun hung high in the sky, but she still shivered. It wasn't often that she was alone in the clinic like that without at least someone there with her.

There was only one way to make sure. She needed to open the door.

Whitney never really thought of herself as brave. Actually, truth be told, she was likely about as far from brave as a person could get. But this was stupid. She'd let herself fall prey to silly thoughts. People did not try and break into places in the middle of the morning in broad daylight. It'd make far more sense to break in when no one was there if they wanted to steal any drugs.

She slowly opened the door, her hand ready on the phone.

She swung the door wide and looked around.

Nothing.

Little Hank sat beside her, staring down the alley as if he were seeing something she wasn't. The feeling unnerved her, but still, there was nothing there. Even the best criminals needed to be there to actually steal anything.

"Let's finish up, boy," she said a little louder than she needed to. "Lisa will be here soon."

Whitney shut the door and locked it quickly.

She leaned against the door and took in deep breaths. The whole thing was silly. No one was there. If someone had been there, she would have seen them. She wondered if she was still just a bit off from the previous night's drinking. It was the heaviest partying she'd done in a while.

The phone in her pocket buzzed, and she pulled it out.
Be there in 10.

Whitney shook her head and smiled.

"Come on, Hank," she said to the little dog. "We better hurry."

* * *

Cage was beyond tired of sitting in his cramped little car. Never in his life did he think he'd feel that way, but that was all before his knee. Now it just felt like torture. His legs were too long, and he had to keep his knee bent for far too long.

"Not much action," Trent said and looked over at him.

Cage wasn't really sure what the other man was hoping to see, but the place was dead.

"How many men in the gang?" Trent asked.

Cage stared across the way through the brush they were parked behind.

"Maybe thirty or forty guys." He shrugged.

Trent continued to watch the shop across the way. "That many and it's this quiet?" he said, almost to himself.

Cage perked up a little. He hadn't really thought of it that way. With that many guys, they should have seen at least a little movement.

"What are you thinking?" Cage asked the ex-SEAL.

Trent looked back over to him. "I'm thinking there's something going on for sure now. No way this place is going to be this quiet with that many men."

A young boy, barely a teenager if that, walked alongside the road, and they watched as he entered the shop from the side.

"Who's that?" Trent asked.

Cage remembered the kid. The boy had taken his and Ryder's guns when they visited Carlos before the mountain fires and shoot-outs.

"He's harmless," Cage said, slightly uncomfortable remembering the man who had given his life to save a man he hardly knew. "He's Carlos's grandson."

Trent narrowed his eyes. "He work there?"

Cage shrugged. "Did the last time I saw him."

Trent ran a hand along the back of his neck. "Might be able to get some information from him."

Cage shook his head. The idea of talking to the grandson

of the man who died for him was way beyond his comfort zone. He wasn't sure.

"He didn't know shit last time," Cage said. "I doubt things have changed. He's just a kid. Not like they are going to key him in on anything important, especially after what Carlos did."

Trent nodded. "Well, maybe we should pay Charlie a visit," he said. "See if he knows where they might be going."

Cage shrugged. Wasn't like he had much else to do, especially since Reed had forced him out.

Trent pulled out his phone and started the car.

"Now, let's get you to that appointment," Trent said with a smile.

Something churned in Cage as he felt his resolve slip.

CHAPTER SIX

LUNCH WAS A LITTLE LESS BUSY in the cafeteria than it normally was on the weekend, which was when she mainly volunteered to help with the dogs and other therapy animals they trained in the building.

Normally that wouldn't have been a big deal for Whitney, but today was the day Ted had decided to ambush her with something she wasn't ready for. Well, ambush was a bit unfair. It's not like she hadn't seen this coming.

"I think we can be something special," Ted said with a soft smile. "We've been hanging out, but I'd like to take it to the next level. Start dating, not just having coffee."

She looked across the table to the man sitting there and sighed. It wasn't that he wasn't good-looking. Ted was neat and wore button-up shirts. He was the kind of guy that parents hoped their daughter would date. Ted had a great job at his well-established vet office, and people loved him.

Whitney glanced back down at her salad when she realized she'd been staring too long.

Really, the only problem with Ted was that there was nothing there. She didn't want to quote her mother, but there just wasn't any spark. Nothing burned. Nothing even hinted at burning.

She stiffened a little at the thought. Maybe the spark was just her subconscious trying to protect her. After all, people who gave off that spark were people she couldn't trust. People who went home with boob-zillas and acted all innocent and like they just wanted to be with one person when they were still secretly players. No. That wasn't what she wanted. She needed something else, someone else.

Still, she glanced up to Ted again. Lisa had been right. Ted was a nice guy, and jerking him around wasn't what she wanted to do either. Couldn't she just learn to have that spark for him?

Deep down she knew that wasn't going to happen. It was unfair to both of them to continue to drag this thing out.

"Whitney?" Ted said, staring at her, waiting for an answer that she wouldn't be able to give.

She shook her auburn hair.

"I'm sorry," she said, giving him a small smile. "I'm just not ready for that."

His face fell, and she knew that wasn't the answer he was expecting.

"Listen, Ted," she said, leaning forward. "I just don't know if I'll ever be ready."

He frowned a little.

She knew it sounded silly, a bit too much like, 'It's not you, it's me,' but she really didn't have a better answer. Her feelings for him weren't likely to ever be more than platonic, and the person who she did feel something for would likely break her heart. A rock and a nice, soft place. It was ironic that after all this time, she'd still end up like her mother. She'd ended up in love with love and chasing the wrong sort of man. Well, not if she could help it.

"I'll wait," he said suddenly, pulling her from her dark thoughts.

Whitney blanched at the statement.

"Wait?" she asked, hoping that maybe she had misunderstood.

Ted nodded. His perfect brown hair bobbed a little but still managed to keep its shape.

"If you need time, I can give you that." He smiled warmly at her and took her hand. "I understand this sort of thing can be intense."

This wasn't going like she planned at all.

"We could be good for each other," he said quietly. "If you just gave us a chance."

She didn't really know what to say, but it wasn't really the kind of confession that most girls wanted to hear. Even someone like her wanted more.

Whitney pulled her hand back and shook her head.

"I think you're a great guy, Ted, but I can't let you wait for me," she said and looked down at the salmon sitting on top of her salad. It didn't look like she'd get the chance to eat it now.

Ted sat up suddenly, knocking the table as he did so and dragging her attention back to him.

"I'll wait," he said firmly. He nodded, more to himself than anything.

Whitney swallowed. There was no convincing him now. It was odd how the thing she had most admired in him, his determination, was now coming to bite her in the ass.

"Ted, I really don't think it will make a differ—"

She stopped at the sight of Lisa rounding the corner.

"There you are," her friend said, grinning at her. "You won't believe who I just saw."

Whitney frowned a little, both at the interruption and the giddy expression on her friend's face.

"Who?" She raised a brow.

Lisa grinned and sat in the chair next to her.

"Cage."

* * *

So the trip to the dog therapy place hadn't been as bad as he'd expected. The people that worked at the therapy place were nice, and no one acted like he couldn't do things for himself. Actually, they had gone out of their way to say that the dogs were just there to make things easier. It seemed like they got him, understood he wasn't done just because his knee had been shot.

Cage still wasn't convinced, but it wasn't a bad option, especially if his knee disability was going to be long-term. His stomach twisted at the thought, but it wasn't impossible. The last time he'd seen the doctor, he had said it would be a miracle if Cage regained full mobility. Though he'd also said that his recovery had been pretty amazing, and that gave Cage hope. Maybe it shouldn't have, but it did.

"So what do you think?" Mark asked.

He liked the carefree ex-military man who had taken the time to show them around. Trent had been right. Mark was easygoing and never once pushed anything on him. It was like talking to one of the guys at work, except with less random busting his balls bullshit.

Cage rubbed the back of his neck.

"I'm going to be honest," he said. "I'm just not sure I'd need a dog long-term."

Mark frowned a little. "But your doctor was willing to write a script for a therapy dog? Your doctor knows your long-term medical needs."

Mark and Trent exchanged looks, and Cage knew what that meant. They thought he was in denial.

"Look, I'm just not sure where things are going," he said and moved slowly down the hall to the front door. It had been a nice visit, but he was ready to be done. He didn't want any pressure to start coming. "I'd just like to think on it a bit more. It's a big decision."

Mark nodded and smiled. "I understand," he said, stopping at the front desk. "It is a big step, but just keep thinking on it. This isn't something you have to do right now. We'll be here."

Cage took his hand and nodded. It might not be a step he was ready to take, but that didn't mean that it wouldn't happen someday. He couldn't say for sure what the future would hold.

"While I have you," Mark said, glancing nervously to Trent and then back to him, "have you considered what a dog might do to help your PTSD?"

Cage clenched his fist and glared at Trent.

"I haven't been diagnosed with PTSD," he said through gritted teeth.

Trent looked away.

Mark gave a weak smile. "We see a lot of guys like you, and dogs are always good companions."

Cage grunted. They acted like he was going to crack any second. Besides, it wasn't like he'd been through war and suffered like Trent. He could hardly qualify for something so serious.

"Thanks for the tour," Cage said tightly and moved to the door. "I'll keep what you said in mind."

He pushed through hard, ignoring Trent behind him.

"I'll get the car," Trent said quietly.

Cage grunted. Everything in him wanted to deny the option to pick him up, but there was no way he could make it to the car now. After being cramped in one position too long and then walking around so much, his knee was throbbing.

"You just don't know when to quit, do you?" a woman said.

Her voice cut through the air, and he knew instantly she was talking to him.

Whitney placed her hands on her hips and glared at him.

"Whitney?" Ted said from behind her.

Ted and Lisa stared at her as if she had lost her mind, and maybe she had, but this was going too far. Cage's fragile ego could go fly away for all she cared. He didn't get to follow her around just because she saw through his playboy act and blew him off.

"I'm fine," she said to them. "I'll be inside in a second. I just need to have a chat with a certain someone."

Lisa quickly made her way in, but Ted lingered, looking almost uncertain if he should leave her. The two men stared at one another, and she wondered if maybe she was starting something. She certainly didn't want to see Ted hurt.

"Let me know if you need any help," Ted said to her and then turned back to glare at Cage.

Cage snorted. "I'm sure she will."

First, her clinic, then the club and now here. The nerve of that man. Like she needed to answer to him. He didn't own her just because he wanted her.

She watched Ted go inside before continuing.

"You think you can just show up and what?" She waved a hand at him. "I'm supposed to fall all over you? You must just not be used to women saying no to you, huh?"

Cage stared back at her, his mouth open in shock at her anger. It was a first to see him surprised like that, and she liked that she was able to get the drop on him this time, that she could regain some control.

She stepped a little closer.

"Have fun last night?" she asked with a little more venom than she intended. It only proved to her how much it had stung to see that other woman wrapped around him. She'd let Cage get under her skin in both a good and bad way.

He looked away as if he had something to hide. "It's not what you think," Cage said and moved closer to her.

She stepped back. There was no way she was letting her guard down around him. The last time she had, his tongue had found its way into her mouth.

"I'm sure," she said and crossed her arms. "Well, it doesn't matter anyways what you did with boob-zilla. You could have done it all night for all I care."

She turned and walked to the doors.

"Stay away from me and my clinic. I have no interest in

you or anything you think you have to offer," she said.

Her words stung. She could see it in his face, and something in her felt the pain she was dealing. But she had already gone too far. It was too late to turn back.

"Whitney," he said quietly. "Let me explain. You don't understand."

She shook her head and turned around. "If you have to explain, it means you've done too much. I don't have time for this. Goodbye, Cage."

She hurried back inside the cafeteria to where Lisa was waiting. She was glad to see that Ted had moved on. She didn't think she'd be able to face him like this. What she felt for Cage was more than she wanted to admit, even to herself.

"What was that all about?" Lisa asked quietly.

Whitney shook her head. "I just can't deal with him."

Loud music thumped outside, and she looked at the window.

In horror, she watched as Cage slowly made his way to the passenger door and climbed in awkwardly. She didn't know how she hadn't noticed before.

"His leg's messed up," she said. She gasped. It's not like she hadn't seen a lot of wounded guys, particularly vets, in the building. It was the best place in the city to get a therapy dog after all.

"Shit," she groaned. "I am so stupid sometimes."

Lisa patted her on the back.

"Yes, yes, you are."

CHAPTER SEVEN

CAGE LET THE LOUD ROCK MUSIC pumping through his ear-buds fill his head and drown out the words from earlier.

He'd royally fucked up, and this time, it wasn't even his fault. That was the real kicker.

His leg burned as he pressed hard against the leg weight. He had to get it working right. There wouldn't be any chance of a return to his life before if he didn't.

Sweat ran down the side of his head as he pushed hard against the weight. He could do this. He could push through the pain, and it would build the muscle. The bullet took his strength from him, but he could get it back.

Whitney leaned over him.

He jumped. All the strength in his leg gave out as his concentration was lost. Pain tore through him, and he grunted.

She frowned at him, her face upside down as he lay against the bench.

Cage closed his eyes for a moment as he tried to focus his way through the pain and the surprise. The workout room at the security firm was about the last place he expected to see her. His leg started to throb.

When he opened his eyes, she was no longer standing over him. He blinked, wondering if he'd just been seeing things, but that made no sense. Sure, his leg hurt, but not enough to make him hallucinate.

He jumped as something cold touched his knee. He sat up quickly.

Whitney said something, but he couldn't make it out. He

realized that she was indeed truly there, and he still had the music blasting in his ears.

"What?" he asked and popped the headphones out.

"Shouldn't you be resting it?" she said and pointed to his knee. She'd squatted to place the ice pack.

Cage turned his head. It wasn't often that he was embarrassed, but having her talk so directly about his leg made him irritated. He'd done everything he could to keep her from finding out, and now she knew. He didn't want or need her pity.

"How did you get in?" he asked, not really certain what to do.

Seeing her was about the last thing he expected, especially there.

Whitney nodded to the door. "Trent let me in," she said. "He said to let you know he'll be back later to get you."

She blushed a little, but he tried not to read anything into it. Last night he'd wanted so much more, and it didn't happen. Everything had gone to shit instead.

"Cage," she said quietly.

He couldn't make himself look at her.

Her thumb brushed the tender skin along his knee and traced the scar there. He turned quickly. There was no escaping her seeing the scar. Even with the wrap, his knee poked through the hole, revealing the bright, puckered scar.

"It's warm," she said quietly. "You shouldn't push it so hard."

Cage glared at her as his heart thumped in his ears.

"I don't know what it matters to you," he said quietly. "You already made that clear."

He hated his voice, hated the whine that came out as he tried to push down all the insecurities he felt. She needed to respect him as a man, and whining wasn't the way to achieve that.

"I didn't know," she said quietly.

"And if you had known?"

He stared at her, not really sure if he wanted to hear the answer.

Whitney chewed on her bottom lip and glanced away.

"I wouldn't have said those things," she said.

Cage leaned forward and stared at her. When he stood suddenly, she gasped and leaned back.

"It's fine," he said and walked over to the lockers, ignoring the pain in his knee.

Whitney frowned at his retreating back. For a second, she had thought he was going to kiss her.

"Fine?" she said, following him.

He pulled open the door to a locker and retrieved a bottle of water from the inside. She watched as he gulped down the contents. His neck moved to swallow, and she fixated on the firm line of his neck. The sight made her beyond thirsty.

A droplet of water leaked from the side of his mouth and trailed down his neck before disappearing into the collar of his shirt. She could see the water trailing down his body over his pecs in her mind.

She bit her lip, trying to clear her thoughts.

"Want a drink?" he said.

He gave her a cocky smile, and she blushed at getting caught.

Whitney shut her mouth and shook her head.

"Sure?" he asked and placed the bottle close to her mouth.

As silly as it was, she tried not to think about how his mouth had just been on it.

"I'm good," she said.

Cage paused for a moment before putting the bottle back on the shelf.

Whitney heaved a sigh of relief.

"I just wanted to say—" she said, stopping as he reached

down for the hem of his shirt. "What are you—"

It was over his head before she could even get the question out.

A smattering of hair covered his wide and muscled chest. Her fingers twitched to run along the hard planes.

"Whitney?" he said.

She had no idea what he was asking. She looked up at him but couldn't even form what to say.

Her eyes fell back to his chest. She licked her lips and tried to find something other than all the gorgeous skin in front of her to concentrate on. Was he purposefully messing with her?

She jumped when Cage slammed the locker closed. His eyes were fixed on her, and the same burn as the previous night swept through her, threatening to consume her.

He took a step closer and she backed up.

"Why didn't you let me take you home yesterday?" he asked. His voice was low and hit a tone that made her nipples pebble under her white blouse.

"I—I," she stammered. She looked back up at him and tried to find what little piece of sense she could maintain. "You seemed busy."

He nodded and moved a step forward.

"I wanted to be busy with you," he said.

She shook a little as she stepped back a bit more. Something about the way he spoke pulled her body toward him.

"I don't think your friend would have liked that," she said and glanced around.

Despite the hope that someone might pop in, she knew it was dead in the building. Trent had so much as told her so. The men were all out in the field or at home.

"I don't give a fuck what Sheryl wants," he said roughly. "I didn't want her and told her as much. Several times."

Whitney swallowed hard. The backs of her feet reached the wall behind her. Her heart started to pound.

Cage moved a little closer.

Whitney watched him, not really sure what she wanted. A part of her wanted to run and get away from him before she risked too much. But a larger part wanted to just give in like she had the night before. Her body wouldn't let her deny that the spark was there.

She looked down at his chest and then back up to his face.

"Was that your boyfriend?" Cage asked. He placed his hand against the wall by her head.

Whitney turned the other way and huffed. Despite her traitorous body, she wasn't about to give Cage easy satisfaction.

He brought his other hand to the side of her face and pulled it back to where she was staring at him once again.

Whitney tried to breathe, but the air around her seemed thin and made her lungs ache.

"I don't…" she started but stopped as he continued to look at her. "No," she whispered. "I just have coffee with Ted. He's a friend, nothing more."

She silently cursed herself. Why had she told him that?

Cage moved a little closer. His body pressed lightly against hers.

"He wants you," Cage said. His voice was rough, and she wondered if he was trying to hold back. "I could see it in his eyes."

"Ted wants more," she said. Her body trembled as she spoke.

"Tell me you don't want him," Cage said. The hand that had been on her cheek trailed down her side and wrapped around to the dip in her back. She gasped as he pulled her tightly against him. The outline from his gym shorts was hard to miss.

Cage tilted his head down a little more. Whitney stared at him through half-closed eyes, her lust beginning to cloud her thoughts.

"Tell me, Whitney," he said.

She licked her lips, trying not to remember the searing kiss from last night but somehow unable to think of anything else.

"I don't want him," she whispered.

"Good," he said.

His hot mouth attacked her own. Unlike the tender sweet kiss from last night, this one was hungry. She moaned against his mouth and rested her hands against his hot chest. She never knew that just running her hands along a man's chest could excite her so much.

Cage deepened the kiss as her hands explored his well-defined muscles. She grazed his nipple with her nail and jumped when his hands reached down to grip her ass. His thick length pushed hard against her. She tilted her head back and gasped as his mouth worked its way down her neck. Cool air chilled her as he left wet marks on her heated flesh.

"Cage," she whispered. Her voice sounded strange, far away, as if it weren't even her own.

When his hand slid along the bare skin of her leg, Whitney's eyes shot open.

This was going to happen. She was going to let him touch her in the middle of his work place, in the middle of a gym.

The moment his hand slipped into her panties, all those thoughts vanished. All that mattered was his gentle finger sweeping back and forth over her wet center.

Whitney gripped his arms and panted as Cage rubbed her aching clit with his miraculous fingers. He slowly circled her, drawing out little sounds she didn't even know she could make.

Her nails bit into his arms, but she couldn't seem to stop. She was so close to release.

"Shit," Cage grunted near her ear. She could feel him tremble. It matched her own body.

Whitney cried out as he pressed hard against her clit. The pressure she wanted was there. He rubbed back and forth against her, pushing a finger into her with each stroke.

It was maddening. The more he rubbed, the more she wanted to feel him in her. Deep. So deep that when she came, he'd be able to feel her squeezing him.

The more those thoughts filled her head, the more excitement built in her. This wasn't her. She didn't think those kind of things. But at that moment, there was nothing else she wanted more.

"Now," Cage said. His voice was strained as he pushed two fingers deep inside.

Whitney came crashing over the edge. She cried out against his shoulder and breathed heavily through the rolling waves of pleasure. Every now and again, Cage would curl his fingers, causing a new ripple.

Sweat beaded on her brow as Whitney pulled herself back from bliss.

It was only then that she noticed how badly he was shaking.

"Cage," she said quickly. The tremors from earlier still rippled inside her. "Maybe you should sit."

"I'm fine," he said quickly, trying to keep the irritation out of his voice.

He sure as hell wasn't fine, but there was no way he could say that. How the hell was he going to make love to her if he couldn't even stand to put pressure on his leg long enough for her to get off? Pathetic.

"It's really okay," she said.

He could feel himself bristle at her concern. That wasn't what he wanted. Hearing her moan his name as she came on his fingers, that's what he wanted. Only this time he'd like it to be his dick and maybe spend the rest of the night repeating that fun.

"It's fine really," she said and urged him over to the bench. "Maybe we can just rest for a minute."

Anger lanced through him, and he pulled away. The cold air between them helped dampen the irritation.

"I'm good," he said and turned his back.

He heard her rustling behind him but stayed the way he was. She couldn't see him like this, shaking and pale from pain. It made him weak.

"Well," she said, "I think I'll be going now."

He turned quickly as her heels clicked on the floor.

Cage gritted through the pain to catch up with her.

"Wait," he called out.

She stopped at the door but didn't turn around.

All the ease from earlier had disappeared. Tension lined her back, and he bit back his irritation with himself.

"Whitney," he started but stopped when she turned around.

"I don't understand you, Cage," she said. "What do you want with me? Is this some sort of joke? Am I just another notch after all?"

He shook his head and paled at her words. She was just talking to him, and there he went fucking it up.

"It's not like that," he said. "I like you."

The world around them went silent as she stared back at him in disbelief.

"What?"

He took in a deep breath. "You're different," he said and looked away. Talking about his emotions wasn't something he was very good at. "I want us to get to know each other better."

The sight of Whitney crossing her arms drew his attention back, and he swallowed.

"Know each other better?" she said, raising a brow. "And we do that by having sex?"

"No…" He stopped when she scowled. "Yes." Cage

sighed. Things weren't going at all like he hoped. "Can't we do both?"

Whitney shook her head. "I don't work that way," she said. "Sex isn't something that just happens. It means something to me. I need to know things before I jump into bed with someone."

She sighed and turned back toward the door.

"I just don't think I'm the woman for you, Cage."

A lump formed in his throat as she disappeared out the door.

CHAPTER EIGHT

WHITNEY'S EYES STUNG as she stepped away from the door into the darkness. There was no way she should feel bad, and yet there she was.

She took a deep breath. The recent rain made for cool nights, and it helped fight off the tears that were very close to falling.

"No."

Her heart leapt into her throat at the sound of Cage behind her.

She picked up her pace to get to her car.

"There is no way in hell I'm letting you get away with that," he said and kept pace with her. She knew his leg had to be killing him after standing on it for so long and now chasing after her.

"Cage," she said, not looking at him. Only a few more steps and she'd be at her car. Then she could drive away and leave this whole mess behind her. "Just let it go."

Strong hands spun her around as she reached her door, and once again she found herself pinned against Cage and something hard.

"There is no fucking way I'm letting things go after the way you just kissed me." He leaned in, and his hot breath spread out across her face and made her shiver. "Not after the way you came for me," he whispered. "We are so not done. I know that, and you know that."

Her nipples tightened, and she cursed them for betraying her like that.

"I just don't think…" she said and groped around for the handle of the car. "I just don't think we're a good idea. I'm not saying I'm not attracted to you, but I go on more than just attraction."

She nearly jumped for joy when she finally found the open loop to pull.

"I'm not buying it," he said quietly. "I'm going to show you—"

He stopped as something clattered against the ground and jingled as it bounced.

They looked down at the shiny object.

"Bracelet?" Cage asked as he knelt down to pick it up.

Whitney shook her head.

He opened his large hand, and she frowned.

"A collar?" she said.

They looked up and down the street, as if some lost dog might pop out of nowhere. She didn't recognize the collar.

Something inside her twisted as she stared at the sparkly little rhinestone collar. She'd seen so many collars in her time as a vet, but she had never felt so odd about one.

She gasped as her mind finally processed what she was seeing.

"This collar was cut off," she whispered.

* * *

Cage paced the meeting room as he tried to think. None of this made sense.

"Is this a dog you know?" Trent asked Whitney as she sipped on some hot tea to calm her nerves.

Cage stopped to look at her.

Her hands trembled as she shook her head.

"Not that I can remember," she said quietly. "I'd have to look it up, but it's rare that I don't know one of my animals, and that's a pretty distinctive collar."

Cage believed her. She cared about the animals that came into her clinic. He knew that to be true from the follow-up calls Meg had received. Even after Harley had totally healed, Whitney called just to check in.

"What about enemies?" Trent asked.

Whitney stared blankly at him.

If Cage had to guess, she likely didn't even know how to have an enemy. It wasn't exactly like veterinarians made the kind of enemies that security contractors did.

"I don't think I have any enemies," she said quietly.

"Any troublesome pet owners?" Cage said.

She looked over to him, and the corner of her mouth twitched.

"One or two," she said. He was glad to see that she was starting to snap out of the initial shock.

He stared at the collar in her hand and scrubbed his face but stopped when he caught her staring at him. She chewed her lip nervously.

"I did hear a noise this morning," she said. "I didn't think anything of it at first, but now I'm not sure."

The hairs on the back of his neck stood as she spoke.

"A noise?" Trent asked.

Whitney nodded, and her auburn hair bobbed around her face.

"It sounded like someone was on the other side of the door," she said. "Hank got nervous. When I went to look, though, no one was there."

Cage frowned. "Who's Hank?"

She looked up at him and smiled. "A beagle puppy that's on the mend."

Cage nodded. It was silly. He didn't even have claim on her, and yet he was ready to beat the shit out of anyone that looked at her the wrong way.

Trent shrugged. "It could just be chance."

Cage frowned and shook his head. "It would be too coincidental, and there's no such thing in our line of work."

Whitney sighed. The fear in her big green eyes was almost too much for him.

"Should I be worried?" she whispered.

"Worried? No." He stepped over to her. He would have loved to get down to where she was and look her in the eye, but there was no way his knee would allow it. "You do need to be cautious," he said firmly.

She nodded and stood. "I need to go," she said quietly. "I've still got to let Hank out."

Cage shook his head. There was no way he was going to let her go there without cover. If some freak was after her, she'd need protection.

"Let's go, then," he said and looked over to Trent, who nodded.

"Oh, I can't let you—" she began.

Cage walked over to her and stood tall in front of her. "We're going," he said firmly but leaned down when a hard line formed on her face. "I need to keep you safe," he whispered. "That's the way I am."

Her eyes softened, and he signed inwardly. After everything that happened tonight, this was a win.

* * *

Whitney cursed herself as she walked from cage to cage, making sure the animals had what they needed. There weren't as many she'd had recently, thankfully, but there were still enough to make checking on them quite a task.

Fortunately, most were on the mend and only needed minor care.

Hank barked from his cage and danced around.

She couldn't help but laugh as his little butt wiggled around in the cage.

Whitney opened the front latch and watched as he shot

out of the confined space toward Cage, who stood silently a bit in front of the opened door, the night shrouding him slightly.

"Hank?" he said as he stooped to pet the little pup.

She smiled as Hank wiggled his way onto his back for a belly rub.

"He just seemed so wise when he came in," she said quietly. "I thought he needed a grownup name."

Cage laughed at the little dog. "Well, he's about as grownup as a tadpole."

She shook her head and moved to the door that opened to the small courtyard.

"He didn't seem that way when he came in," she said and watched as Hank darted out into the yard. "Dirty, tired and injured, he just seemed broken."

Cage grunted, and she turned to look at him.

"Looks like he's made a full recovery," he said.

She nodded and looked away. Something about the way the conversation was going made her uncomfortable. After all the ups and downs that evening, she wanted to avoid any more emotional minefields.

"Animals are amazing," she said and stared out at the blur of Hank darting around in the darkness outside. "I've seen them come back from things, even better than they were before. Think about Harley."

Cage nodded. After a moment, he placed a hand on her shoulder, and she shivered at the touch.

"People can come back stronger, too," he said quietly.

She turned to look at him. His eyes were shrouded in darkness, but she knew he was staring at her.

"Cage," she said.

"Give me a chance," he said and stepped a little closer. "Give me the same chance you gave Hank."

"It's not the same," she said.

Whitney pulled away.

"Being shot wasn't the worst thing that happened that day," Cage said.

Whitney stilled and stared up at the quiet man.

"The worst was watching him die to protect me," Cage said. His voice cracked as he spoke, and she knew the emotion was raw.

"Who died?" The words were out before she could even stop them.

"Carlos," he said quietly. "He stepped in front of me. I should be the one dead in the ground."

She shivered at the thought and stepped closer. "Don't say that."

Her voice was harsh and filled with emotion she didn't know was buried in her.

"I'm glad you're here," she said quietly and stepped a little closer. "I'm glad it wasn't you."

Cage stared back at her for a moment and then slowly leaned down. She had time to step away if she wanted. He was giving her all the time in the world to step away, but she didn't want to.

There was more to him than the pretty face, more than the thrill-seeking man she thought was there. Cage was sweet. He was a man who loved animals and fought fiercely to defend the honor of his sister's dog. More than that, he was someone who lived honestly, even if it hurt him.

His lips touched hers, and she sighed. Being wrapped up in his arms felt right, more right than she'd ever experienced.

It wasn't a deep kiss. He didn't press into her like he had before. The word tender floated through her mind and drifted into love.

She pulled back and tried not the think about the L word. That was not something she could get behind. Things like that happened in fairytales. Standing outside while the dog peed, hoping that her life wasn't in danger, was not a fairytale.

"Go out with me," Cage said. His words cut into her

thoughts and knocked her stability around a bit.

"A date?" she asked.

"Let me get to know you," he said. His voice sounded surer than before. "Let me show you that I can be more than what you think I am."

Whitney opened her mouth and then closed it.

A date.

It seemed like the title of a horror movie.

"Yes."

Whitney didn't even know where that came from. She opened her mouth to say no, and a yes came out.

Cage grinned at her.

"Yes," he repeated her answer, and a weight lifted off her.

"Hank," she called out into the darkness. The little guy raced to them and again danced around Cage.

They stepped in, and she closed the door. His hand came over hers as she slipped the lock in place.

"Tell me you want to," he said. His voice was serious. "That you aren't just doing this because you feel sorry for me."

Whitney snorted. "Sorry for you?" she said and moved further into the room. "Yes, I feel really sorry for the super-sexy security guy."

The room grew quiet, and she hoped that she hadn't crossed the line.

When she turned to look at him, he was grinning from ear to ear.

"You think I'm super sexy?" he laughed.

She could feel the heat on her face as it spread to her whole body.

"I, I," she stammered. "I need to get Hank home."

Cage picked up the little pup, who only tried to dance in his arms.

"She thinks I'm sexy," he whispered.

Whitney rolled her eyes and turned away. "Are you done

yet?" she tossed over her shoulder.

Cage laughed and followed her to the front door. When they were on the other side, he continued following her to the car. He held up a hand to Trent, who flashed the lights.

Whitney had to admit, even when he was off, he was still on.

"When?" Cage said and placed Hank into the back.

Whitney stared at him, confused.

"Our date," he said quietly. "When should we have it?"

Her mind blanked.

"Friday?" he suggested.

Whitney nodded. Her mind blanked again as he leaned in to kiss her. This time was brief but just as intense as every other time.

"Friday," she whispered as she climbed into the car. Now she'd have all week to freak out about what a bad idea dating Cage Allen was.

CHAPTER NINE

CAGE FROWNED from his seat at the conference table.

"I'm telling you there's something weird going on with her," he said to Reed.

Cage's older brother stared at him with his green eyes and shook his head.

"It's not enough to go on, and you know it," Reed said. "Lots of weird stuff happens to people."

Cage turned his head to look to Trent. "I don't know it."

Reed sighed and sat down in his chair. The other men in the room had grown quiet watching them, but Cage didn't give a shit. His brother was wrong, and if that meant being called out in front of everyone, then so be it.

"What I do know," Cage said, looking over to Ryder, "is that we had enough manpower for someone to roll by Irene's place when she needed it."

Sure, maybe it was a bit cheap, but it was still true.

Ryder frowned and turned away.

"That was before the shit hit the fan," Reed said, drawing his attention back to him. "We just don't have the manpower to spare. We're stretched about as thin as we can manage. If we don't get the drop on the Los Malos, then they will get the drop on us. I just can't have that. They've already shown how fucking crazy they are."

Cage snorted. "And you've been getting vital information recently?"

Reed grew quiet and pressed his lips together.

"We're doing what we can," he said quickly.

"Great," Cage said and moved forward. "So where are the Los Malos going during the day?"

The room grew still. This was a direct challenge, and it was clear that he meant business.

"We're not sure, but it seems like they've taken a majority of their business off their grounds," Reed said tightly. "They were doing some work last night on one of their buildings on site. We're still piecing it all together."

He looked around the room, and Cage knew that the fight was over.

"We think they are getting ready to move whatever they are doing to their land," Reed said.

"That seems a little stupid," Kace said and leaned back. "If the PD gets wind of this, then it's all over."

Reed nodded. "This is why we think they must have things looking on the up and up. Hide in plain sight."

Ryder snorted. "And don't forget that there are some in the department who would be fine taking a little extra cash on the side to make it look legal. Plus, with a lot of the Russian and Kelly Clan shit still going on, it's not like the force isn't spread thin itself."

Cage shook his head. Things were not working out in their favor, and he didn't even know if they would end up that way. With the situation as it currently stood, they would be lucky to figure this shit out before it went south. They needed to surprise the Los Malos, or more people were going to get hurt.

"Ryder, you keep working with Charlie. He's our best guess in all this," Reed said. "But keep it on the down low. Finn is right," he said, looking over to Cage and Trent. "If Charlie can't do business because of us, then we're all fucked. Everyone else, keep up the rotations. I just know they are going to escalate things, and we need to be ready."

The men got up to leave. Reed caught Cage as he was about to slip out the door.

"My office," he said quietly.

Cage frowned. If Reed thought he was going to chew him out over this, he better be ready for one hell of a fight. It's not like Reed and Ryder hadn't risked men from the firm for their women.

They walked down the hall quietly. Trent followed behind, and Cage wondered what was going on.

When they entered the room, Reed closed the door and gestured to a chair.

Cage slipped in with ease and sighed at the room to stretch out.

"I want to know more about this dog situation," Reed said.

Cage frowned, surprised. The impression he'd gotten from his brother in the meeting was totally different.

"What?" Cage said.

Reed took a seat on the other side of the desk.

"We've been getting reports from all over," he said. "Dogs are coming up missing."

Cage frowned. "Dogs?"

Reed shrugged. "It's not really clear to me why this might be happening."

"Then why'd you blow me off in the meeting?"

"Because it could be totally unrelated. Everything I said about us being stretched thin is still true, and I'm not going to commit resources to some wild goose chase without firm evidence."

Cage leaned forward to respond, but it was Trent that spoke first. "Think it's a big ring?"

Reed shrugged. "At the moment, I'm not sure of anything, but like I said I can't spend the man hours on it. Not with the way things stand."

Cage raised a brow. "Then why the hell are you telling me about it?"

Trent sighed. "Because he's not giving out the assignment.

I am."

Cage looked between the two of them. "What the hell is going on?"

"Look," Trent said. "I need something to cut my teeth on in the area. If we find the missing dogs, more money comes in. There's plenty of work here." He shrugged. "I just need to establish myself. Besides," Trent grinned, "I get to watch that vet make you squirm. That's pretty amazing and entertaining."

Cage frowned, flipped off the ex-SEAL and turned back to his brother.

"You cool with this?" Cage asked and shifted in his chair.

All this time he'd been working for his brother. It never occurred to him that he might be taking orders from someone else. He liked and respected Trent, but still, it felt slightly weird.

Reed sighed and scrubbed a hand across his face.

"I'm getting too old to be doing stake-outs all night," he said and leaned back in his chair. Cage had seen that Reed was looking more tired recently, and he wondered if he was just taking on too much. It's not like he was that much older. "Olivia hates when I leave at night, and Violet gets upset when I'm not there to see her in the morning."

Cage frowned. That didn't really sound like much of a problem.

"So start assigning that shit to the men," Cage said. "That's why you have them."

Reed shook his head. "Not enough men to go around. Kace is a mess with Jessica being pregnant. Liam is working with Finn, and Meg wants a baby."

Cage nearly choked at the thought of his baby sister getting pregnant.

"At least Ryder is taking it slow on the baby front, but it won't be long. We all know that having kids changes things. We have to be more careful."

Reed sat up and placed his hands on his desk like he was

prepping himself to say something he didn't really want to.

"Things are growing here," he said quietly. "Our family is growing." He pressed his lips together. "My family is growing."

Cage raised both brows in surprise. "Shit, Olivia's pregnant?"

His heart filled with love at the thought of a new child entering their family.

Reed nodded, but his expression was not even close to the elated look most fathers would have. "It's one of the biggest reasons I asked Trent to come in so soon."

Trent nodded once but remained silent.

Cage leaned forward. All happiness disappeared

"What's going on?" Cage said.

Reed looked at him with such anguish it made his heart ache. "Olivia is sick," he said, his voice was just above a whisper. "Mom's had to watch Violet during the day. This pregnancy has been hard. Very hard."

His stomach twisted at his brother's pain.

"What's wrong?"

Reed took in a breath, and this time spoke with more strength than Cage would have thought possible.

"She's been bleeding," he said. "Right now they want her on bedrest, but she'll eventually have to stay at the hospital. We're just hoping the baby stays in until the lungs are fully formed, but it's definitely going to be premature."

"Shit," Cage said quietly. It had never occurred to him that his brother could be dealing with all this, and he wouldn't know. "Mom knows?"

Reed nodded. Their conversation had drained him, or maybe just dealing with things had drained him.

Cage looked over to Trent, who wore a grim expression.

Trent shook his head. "I didn't know all this when Reed contacted me," he said and looked back at him. "All I knew was that there might be a chance to live near my dad and sister."

Cage nodded and looked back to Reed.

"How long have you been dealing with this?"

Reed looked at the glow of the computer on the side of the desk.

"Just after you were shot," he said after some time.

The room spun a little as Cage took it in. They had been suffering in silence while everyone made sure he was comfortable. The thought didn't sit well with him. Even with a bad knee, he still could support his family.

"Why didn't you say something?" Cage said. "We're family. Everyone would have been there for you. All of you. You know that, right?"

Reed looked over to him. "Olivia wanted to make sure you got what you needed."

The green eyes of their father stared back at him through Reed, and Cage had to look away.

"You've been in a bad place recently," Reed said to him. "No one blames you. This whole thing took something out of you. Hell, I think any of us would feel the same way if it happened to us."

Fear lanced through Cage. He knew they had all suspected that he wasn't the same, but still, he thought he hid it all a little better than that.

"Liv couldn't stand the idea that you might go through this alone. We have each other, but you don't have that," Reed said. The room went quiet.

He understood that his brother wasn't saying anything to hurt him, and yet those words pierced him in a way he hadn't expected.

He was alone, despite all those women he'd been with. All those nights, and yet there he was, alone. So alone that his brother and sick wife didn't want to risk burdening him with another problem to worry about.

Cage cleared his throat before he spoke. Emotion clogged

his throat.

"I'll do what you need me to," Cage said and looked between the two men.

Reed gave a nod. "For now, we're just establishing Trent here. I plan on being more the silent partner in this."

It made sense. Trent would need more men than just himself and Johnny. They would have to get some of the other men to go over, plus establish contacts around town.

"So where do we go from here?" Cage asked the two men.

Reed waved a hand for Trent to take over.

Trent smiled at him. "Well, for now, I think we better see what the hell is going on with your vet."

Cage sighed inside. There was something shady going on, and he had to know she was safe. Maybe he couldn't do much to help out Olivia and Reed with their problem, but protecting Whitney was still something he could manage, even with his knee.

"Good," Cage said. "Let's get started."

Trent nodded to Reed and made his way to the door. Once he was out, Cage turned back to Reed.

"You should tell the others," he said quietly. "We care for one another. It's what we do. Why do you think I've worked for your sorry ass all these years?"

Reed nodded. "We plan on breaking the news at the next dinner."

Cage gave a slight nod. He was going to have to toughen up. The family needed to focus on Olivia. He'd get through his own problems fine. The pity party needed to be over. It was time to buckle down and get some real work done.

CHAPTER TEN

"Hump!" Sharon said from the front for about the fifth time.

Whitney swore under her breath and closed her eyes. One more time and she wouldn't be responsible for her actions.

"So," Lisa said quietly next to her as she glanced out the window, "four nights in a row."

Whitney turned to glare at her. She still wasn't sure how to handle Cage keeping an eye on her. A part of her found it very sweet, but the other part was terrified at the idea a person was out there trying to torment her for some unknown reason.

"What?" Lisa asked innocently enough. "It just shows his dedication."

Sharon snorted from her place behind the desk as she closed out the accounts for the day. Whitney gritted her teeth to keep from leaping over the counter and throttling the older woman. Her receptionist was detail-oriented and good at her job, but on some days, her personality really grated.

"That man is only dedicated to one thing, and I think we all know what it is," Sharon said. Her mouth was pressed so thin there was just a line where her lips should be.

Whitney sighed and continued sweeping the lobby area.

"He's here to make sure I'm safe," she said and jumped when the door chimed open.

"You aren't safe?" Ted said from the door, frowning slightly.

He was still wearing his typical work clothes: button-up

white shirt and black slacks. She had no idea how he kept his clothes so clean and pristine. Dealing with animals, she was never quite sure what would happen. Hazard of the job.

Ted walked in a little further and stared at her with worry.

"I'm fine," she said and smiled.

Ted frowned and glanced over his shoulder. Cage sat in a car across the street, watching the place.

"Then why is he here?" he asked.

Whitney could hear the irritation in his voice but shook her head. This wasn't something she should feel guilty over.

"Cage is just making sure nothing happens in the evening," she said and went back to sweeping.

"He doesn't have to," Ted said and moved in her path.

She looked up at him. He just wanted to be a part of her world outside of the volunteer job, but there was no way it would work other than friends. Plus, Ted was a nice guy, but she doubted he could handle it if some criminal or crazy guy came after her.

"It's fine," she said, moving around him. "Sharon, you can go."

Ted moved to her side and spoke in her ear.

"Let me help you," he said. "You just have to give me a chance."

Whitney sighed. She was so tired. It seemed like no matter where she was, she was always on alert. She hadn't been able to sleep like she should.

She looked out the window toward Cage's car. He watched her closely through the window, and despite his aggressive ways, his presence did make her feel safer.

"Cage does this for a living," she said and looked back to Ted. "I think it's best we leave it up to him."

Ted cleared his throat and stepped back. His face had reddened, and she knew she'd hurt his feelings, but she was just so tired of having to work at everything.

"Yes, well," he said and glanced out the window. "I guess

we can't all make a living through violence."

Whitney opened her mouth to say something about the comment, but Lisa cut her off.

"So, Ted," she said from the spot where she was wiping off a chair. "What are you up to tonight?"

His whole expression changed as he looked back to Whitney.

"I came to see if Whitney had plans on Friday." He beamed at her.

"Damn," Lisa said quietly and went back to scrubbing spots.

"I can't," Whitney said and looked away. "I have plans."

"Oh, surely Lisa won't mind if you cancel," he said. He looked over to Lisa, who was suddenly very interested in the chair on the farthest side of the room. "I was thinking we could take it slow. Maybe just dinner and a movie."

"Ted," Whitney said softly.

"Or just dinner." He shrugged.

"I don't—"

"I'm not picky," he said. His smile was stiff and plastered to his face.

"I can't," she said a little louder than she intended, but he wasn't going to keep talking over her. If he didn't understand the situation, then she'd have to make him understand.

His smile slipped a little, and she felt bad for hurting him.

"It's just a simple date," he said and looked around, somewhat uncomfortable. "No expectations."

Whitney shook her head. There was no way around it. She was going to have to lay it on the line.

"I already have a date, Ted," she said.

He grew quiet, and when she looked up, he was glaring out the window.

"It's him, isn't it?" he asked.

She opened her mouth to respond but closed it. At this point, it wouldn't really matter what she said. He knew and that was all that needed to happen. This was best for both of them really. Ted was a nice guy. He just needed to find someone more compatible and interested.

"Well," he said, stiffening his back. "I guess I was under the wrong impression."

"Ted," she said softly and reached out to him, but he was already headed for the door.

It chimed as he opened it. A small draft from the night slipped in and chilled her.

He looked back from the door.

"I hope you know what you're doing. A man like that will eat you alive." He let the door slam behind him as he walked away.

She resisted a laugh. Ted was right. His words were ones she had said to herself many times over the last few days. Still, she couldn't find the will to cancel the whole thing, and she knew that wasn't only about needing Cage's protection.

Whitney wanted this date. She wanted to see what Cage was really all about.

She glanced out the window and watched as Cage kept his gaze on Ted.

It was strange. She'd spent all her life trying to make sure men were never an issue, and now she had two who were causing nothing but issues.

"Well," Lisa said from the other side of the room. "It could have been worse. Sharon could have been here."

Whitney snorted loudly.

* * *

Cage waited patiently outside in the car. Lisa had just gone home, and it usually wasn't long before Whitney left. He worried that Ted might make a scene, but the guy came and went without too much fuss. Not like he was worried he'd be hard to handle even then.

Cage had to keep watch on the place. Although it might seem a little intrusive, he had to know she was safe at night after the collar incident. When they'd run a match on the ID, it came back as a missing poodle. Nothing was adding up though.

Who would do something like that? It didn't really seem like a Los Malos thing to do. If they wanted to make a threat, there were easier, more direct ways to do that. Gangs liked people to know who were messing with them.

Cage frowned as Whitney came out the door and waved at him.

He slid out of the car and made his way over. He cursed his leg and how slow he still was with it. At least the doctor had finally cleared him to drive. That offered him at least some independence and the ability to do his job without a babysitter.

He reached the door, ready to race into action, but slowed down when she smiled at him.

"I thought you might be more comfortable inside," she said.

He tried not to let the frown reach his face as he made his way in. Why did everyone have to be so concerned with making him comfortable? He could deal.

"Thanks," he grunted, knowing she didn't intend for her words to irritate him.

Whitney locked the door behind her and made her way to the back.

Cage followed and tried not to think of how amazing she looked. Her red hair, which was usually pulled off her face, flowed freely around it. He liked that she was in jeans and a t-shirt. It made her seem more real to him.

"Any trouble today?" he asked, hoping she might elaborate on what happened with Ted. Even though the man looked mad, he didn't seem to have done much, but he could have made some quiet threats.

Whitney glanced over to him as she read through a chart outside of a cage.

"Nothing I couldn't handle," she said and looked quickly back to the charts.

"And Ted?" he said, stepping a little closer. "He didn't seem like he could handle it."

She sighed loudly and hung the chart against the cage.

"He'll be fine." She moved on to the next cage.

Cage nodded. It didn't matter if she told him. What did matter was that Ted left mad, and he had a good idea as to why.

"Whitney," he started. He stopped when something rattled the door at the back of the clinic.

They froze and looked at one another. Cage pulled out his gun and stood next to her.

"Stand back and don't open that door unless you hear me," he whispered in her ear.

She nodded and moved against the farthest wall.

Faster than he'd moved in months, Cage stepped outside and followed the line of the building. Shadows moved across the walls, but he kept his mind clear. In order to see them, Cage was going to need to concentrate.

He crept his way to the corner of the building, ignoring some pain in his knee. A quick glance around surprised him. The back alley behind the clinic was well lit and not the ideal spot for breaking in. Hell, most would have at least thought to throw a rock at the light to mask themselves. Of course, arrogance made criminals do stupid crap all the time, so he couldn't be sure.

The alley was empty, and nothing seemed to be out of place.

Cage made his way to the door.

"Whitney," he said and waited for the door to open.

The door creaked open, and her pale face appeared in the door.

A long piece of string hung down to her face and swung in front of her. He frowned at the sight.

"What's that?" he asked.

Whitney reached up to pull it down. Her hands shook.

"It's a chip," she said quietly.

Cage frowned. "A chip?"

"It's a pet tracking chip."

* * *

Whitney paced the floor. This was wrong. It was so beyond wrong.

She looked back at the screen. No matter how many times she looked at the scanned chip, it still came up the poodle.

"Is there a chance it's a mistake?" Cage asked.

She shook her head. "No," she said. "I just can't understand what it's doing outside the dog."

Cage shrugged. "Maybe the dog was rechipped."

She shook her head again. "It's not like that," she said. "Most vets won't even think about taking these out."

"Why?" he asked and settled on the stool in front of the computer.

"It's complicated," she said but could see he wanted more. "The procedure is difficult, and that's just hoping that it's there right under the skin."

"And if it's not?" Cage asked.

She swallowed. It wasn't something she wanted to think about.

"If not, then they have to dig. It can be painful and might cause muscle damage."

Cage grunted. She knew he would understand the gravity of the situation.

She jumped when he suddenly stood and took her hands in his.

"We'll catch this guy," he said quietly. "I don't know what

his game is yet, but we'll catch him."

She nodded. Tears prickled her eyes, and she struggled to keep in control.

As if he couldn't take it any longer, Cage wrapped her in is arms.

Whitney breathed in deeply and tried to get her emotions in check. She was safe. They all were.

"Let's get you home," he rumbled in her ear.

She nodded, still against his chest. It took a few more moments for her to step away, and when she did, all she wanted to do was return to the safety of his arms.

Cage shuffled her to the front door and walked quietly to her car. She liked that he didn't feel the need to fill the silence. Sometimes she just needed to have quiet.

When they came to her car, her heart started to pound.

It hadn't even occurred to her that he might kiss her again.

Whitney opened the door but stopped to turn and look at him.

Cage scanned the area constantly. Watching him ready to protect her made him even more amazing. Whatever his past with women, when it came to his job, he was a consummate professional.

He looked down at her, and all the desire from the last few days bubbled inside her.

"Goodnight," he said.

She closed her eyes, expecting a kiss.

He softly kissed her lips, never going further than a sweet goodbye.

When he pulled back, Whitney opened her eyes.

"Tomorrow," he whispered.

She knew what he meant. It was what she had been waiting for since Sunday. She just hoped there was more than chemistry between them.

She stepped into her car and watched as he got in his.

Tomorrow. She still couldn't quite decide if it was a promise or a threat.

CHAPTER ELEVEN

CAGE CHECKED HIMSELF in the mirror for about the millionth time. He looked like his old self, and that was more than he could say for the last few months. Still, it was strange to see himself like this: hair combed to the side with a crisp button-up shirt and nice jeans. He'd thought about wearing slacks, but it just wasn't something he would normally do on a date. It wasn't his style.

He could do this. This kind of date was something he'd done tons of times before. All he had to do was charm her and show Whitney that he was someone she wanted to get to know better.

Cage came out from the bathroom and found Trent sitting on the couch going over material. Nothing about Whitney's case made any sense. The poodle, chip and collar had been traced two states away. That was a long ways for such a little dog to travel, though admittedly not impossible. What seemed odder was that both the chip and collar would make their way to Whitney of all people.

There was no two ways about it. Something was going on. He just hoped the next move wasn't a dead dog outside her door. He wondered if this case involved the owner of one of Whitney's former patients. People could get attached to their animals for sure, but still, it seemed weird to go through such elaborate trouble, and even if Whitney couldn't save someone's pet, her dedication would have shown through, so Cage had trouble accepting the scenario.

"Any luck?" Cage asked Trent and sat next to him on the

couch.

Trent shook his head.

"Not really," Trent said and looked over at him. "The owner of the poodle said it's been missing for a few days."

Cage frowned. That wasn't near enough time for a little dog to travel hundreds of miles.

"When I started to dig, I found there has been an up-swing in the number of missing dogs in several of the states around us," Trent said. He set down the pages and leaned back on the couch. He rubbed his eyes and frowned.

"What do you think is happening to them?" Cage asked.

Trent shrugged. "Maybe sold for science to shady outfits or just being sold off as pets."

Cage frowned. There were so many things that could be going on. They needed more information.

He sighed and stood.

"Well, the best we can do is keep an eye on the place," Cage said. "Whoever is leaving this stuff for Whitney knows what's going on. I just can't figure out what they are trying to say."

Trent nodded and looked up at him. "You ready for your date?"

Cage grinned and grabbed his keys from the counter.

"I got this," he said and slid his sunglasses on. "This is one area where I have a freaking clue."

When he looked over to Trent, the older man was shaking his head.

"You really think that's going to win her over?"

Cage looked down at himself and then back to Trent.

"What's wrong with the way I look?" Cage frowned.

Trent shook his head.

"Nothing," he said and chuckled. "That is, if you're look-ing for a one-nighter."

Cage looked back down at his clothes. He didn't see what was so bad about his choices. It was the same sort of thing he'd worn on other dates.

"She's not like that," Cage said simply. "It doesn't matter what I wear."

Trent shrugged his shoulders. "Just keep that in mind. She's different. Some of your old instincts might sabotage you a bit."

Cage frowned. He made his way to the door and looked back to Trent.

"She is different," he said more firmly than before. "And I do know that."

He closed the door behind him and made his way to the car. Once in he let the car idle for a moment.

Cage checked himself in the mirror. He looked good. It was the one thing right now that he knew he could do well and he planned on showing her that. Whitney had to see.

He put the car into reverse and backed out of the driveway. He could do this.

* * *

Whitney paced back and forth in her living room.

The date was a bad idea. Everything in her said that it was a bad idea. Getting involved with Cage was just going to get her hurt. Men like him, well, they didn't date women like her, at least not for any length of time. Even if he thought he liked her, he'd get bored. It was his nature. Just like with her father.

She looked at the silver mirror near the door.

Maybe she'd done too much. He hadn't said where they were going, and she wasn't sure how she should dress. She figured a black cocktail dress would be okay for most anything.

Whitney wrung her hands and tried not to think about it. There wasn't time to change how she was dressed even if she wanted to. Cage would be there any second.

She fluffed the curls at the end of her hair and checked her lipstick. It wasn't often that she wore this much makeup. She'd nearly forgotten how to put it on.

The bell rang, and she jumped.

He was out front.

After one last look in the mirror, Whitney smoothed out her dress and answered the door.

She bit down the anxiety tightening her throat and smiled at Cage. Her smile faltered a bit when she noticed his simple button-up shirt and jeans. She'd assumed too much and was way overdressed.

"I didn't know where we'd be going," she started and turned around to go back. "I can change."

Cage reached out and grabbed her hand before she could slip into the back of the house.

"You look amazing," he said and looked her up and down. She shivered at his gaze. "Don't change."

His rough voice made her remember the other night. She didn't know how things were going to end tonight, but she was keeping her options open.

"Okay," she said quietly.

"Ready?" he asked.

Whitney nodded despite the butterflies fluttering around her stomach. She hurried out of the house and quickly closed the door.

"What's the hurry?" he said with a grin.

"I didn't want Hank following me."

"The dog? Why do you have him there and not the clinic?"

She smiled. "He's pretty much healed, and I'm going to provide him some temporary housing."

He nodded, and they continued on to his car.

He held the door open for her as she slipped into the sports car. Never had she thought there was an art to getting into a car, but found out that there must be. The vehicle was so low to the ground she had to reach out and hold the door to steady herself.

Once she was in, he shut the door and made his way around. It was quiet together inside the car. She'd been alone with him several times now, but this seemed so intimate.

"So where are we going?" she asked.

She looked over to him and almost wished she hadn't. His sweet boyish smile beamed back at her.

"I thought we might go shoot pool at a cool place I know and then maybe do a little dancing," he said.

She nodded. Although she wasn't really good at either, it was his date, and she was sure he would make it fun.

They drove in silence. Whitney kept trying to think of something witty to say, but nothing was coming. Instead, all she could do was breathe in his aftershave and think about popping the buttons off his shirt. She squirmed a little in the seat.

"Are you comfortable?" he asked.

Whitney stilled and looked over at him in surprise. She didn't think she was moving that much, but maybe she had been.

"I'm fine," she said. "Thanks."

Cage nodded, his eyes on the road ahead.

"Trent is working on the case," he said after a few moments. "The dog was reported missing a few days ago from a few states over."

Whitney frowned. "How did its stuff get here then?"

Cage shook his head. A piece of hair slipped onto his forehead, and she smiled a little. It was cute and made him look more boyish.

"There's something going on," he said and glanced at her. "Whatever it is, it's focused on you. Right now, all we can do is make sure you're safe."

She nodded. It wasn't something she really wanted to think about, but she was glad Cage was there. Regardless of everything going on and her complicated romantic feelings, she felt safe with him.

Cage stopped the car, and she looked around. This wasn't a side of town she was familiar with. Little bars lined the streets. Loud music poured out of their doors.

She had to stop herself from wrinkling her nose. This was not at all the date she had in mind.

Cage climbed out and opened her door with ease.

He held out his hand, and she took it to get out of the low seat.

She expected that he would let go of her hand once they were out, but he held on.

They made their way inside, and it was clear that Cage liked to come to this place often.

"Been a while," the bartender said to him as they entered.

Cage nodded back.

Whitney looked around, and her expectations were slipping for the evening. It wasn't dirty, but it was more hole in the wall than she was expecting. But maybe she was just being too harsh. It could be tons of fun, and she wasn't giving it a fair chance. She tried to get into the right headspace.

"Hey, baby," a curly-haired brunette said with a serving tray. "Where you been? We missed you."

The woman leaned over the table toward Cage, showing ample amounts of cleavage. Whitney had to look away to keep from saying something she might regret.

"Hey, Candy," Cage said, smiling at the busty woman.

Candy? No, Whitney was sure she wouldn't be able to do this much longer without spouting off something.

"Can you get my date and I a beer?" He looked over to Whitney and smiled. "Want something to eat?"

Candy eyed her with venom, and Whitney pushed herself back into the seat.

She glanced over to Cage.

"I don't know what they have," she said and looked

around for a menu.

Cage waved a hand. "Oh, it's all the usual stuff."

The usual stuff. He said it like she came to places like this all the time.

Cage turned back to Candy. "How about nachos?"

She swallowed and looked away. What about her dress screamed nachos? It wasn't like she wasn't a fan. On a normal night she would be down for some, but not wearing something like this.

The worry that had been eating at her all day grew like a ball in her stomach.

"Should we play a game of pool while we wait?"

She looked up to find Cage standing next to her. He smiled, and she felt the worry ebb a little. Maybe he just didn't think about that sort of thing or thought she would realize they wouldn't be going somewhere fancy. She likely should have thought about it, knowing that he wasn't really the kind of guy to get dressed up.

Whitney smiled and gave him her hand to help her up. She could make this work.

* * *

After the first beer worked through her, Whitney found that she actually liked pool. It wasn't something that she'd ever played before, but it took logic and thinking, something she had in spades.

Not only that, but she was having fun with Cage. He'd taken the time to show her how to hold the cue right and the rules of the game. Much to her surprise, he was patient and didn't get mad when she didn't understand something or made a mistake.

The service from Candy had been less than stellar, and Whitney was pretty sure the bitch had tried to accidentally-on-purpose spill a drink on her, but Whitney had lucked out when a man passing through ended up taking the spill. When the nachos came, she'd had to pretend to eat them, so he wouldn't feel bad, but it was a small sacrifice to have a better date.

Still, she hadn't really gotten to know Cage. Other than the fact he was fun, she didn't know much about him or his plans in life. She might be ready to date him, but that didn't mean much more than that. Granted, it was still further than she'd been willing to go with Ted.

She finished off the last of her beer and set it on the table. Cage grinned at her, and she couldn't help but smile.

"You about ready to go?" he asked.

She nodded.

"Just let me use the restroom real quick," she said.

Cage nodded and took a seat back at the table.

Whitney found the tiny bathroom at the end of a small hall in the back of the building. She slipped in and found there were two stalls.

Not thinking about the cleanliness of the place, she went into the closest.

As she was finishing up, the door creaked open and heels clicked against the floor.

She finished up and found Candy on the other side of the door. The bright red lipstick she was applying stood out on her face.

Whitney turned on the water and washed her hands, trying not to look at the nasty woman. She dried her hands and pulled out the light maroon color she had for her lips.

Her eyes drifted over to Candy, who was fluffing her hair with her fingers.

The woman looked over to her and wrinkled her nose.

"How's the date going?" she asked.

Whitney was somewhat stunned by the question.

"Good," she said. Maybe if she kept it brief, she be able to get out without a cat fight.

"Where you going dancing?" she asked.

Whitney frowned and put down the lip gloss.

"How did you know?" she asked.

Candy laughed loudly at her question.

"What? You think you're the first?" Her red lips curved into a cruel smile. "This is what Cage does."

Whitney took in a deep breath. This woman was just trying to start something. She had been all night.

"I think that dinner and dancing is a pretty common date," Whitney said and went back to looking at herself in the mirror. She tried to steady her hands and ignore the bitter woman.

"I don't think you understand," Candy said and moved a little closer so that she could see her reflection in her own mirror. "This date, this is Cage's way. After dancing, he'll suggest that you take a walk on the pier. Maybe watch the boats roll in. And while you're there, you'll kiss a little."

Whitney swallowed down the bile rising from her stomach.

"He'll suggest that you go back to your place, and when you wake up in the morning, he'll be gone, a sweet note in his place." Candy snorted. "I'm surprised though. Most women know what they're getting with Cage. Guess he can't get the same caliber of woman being such a freak now. I wonder if he can even perform."

Anger boiled in Whitney. This woman just wanted to humiliate her, and there was no way in hell Whitney was going to let her get away with saying something like that.

"Maybe I'll give you a call tomorrow and let you know," Whitney said with a smile and slammed out of the room.

There was no way she was going to let that bitch ruin her date.

Cage sat waiting at the table. It had been a good evening. He was a little surprised when Whitney showed up to the door in such a nice dress and nearly changed plans but was glad he hadn't. Given that it was his first time back at dating, it was good to stick to what he knew. He wanted this to work more than anything, and if that meant going with the plan, that was fine with him. At least he knew it worked.

Whitney stormed out of the bathroom and back into the booth.

Cage frowned and leaned forward a little.

"Something wrong?" he asked.

Whitney took a deep breath and let it out. Her perfume drifted over to him, and he smiled at her.

"I'm fine," she said and took a drink of water.

"Good," he said and reached across to take her hand. He stroked the tender skin of her wrist against his calloused thumb. "I was thinking…" He swallowed and looked over to her bright green eyes. "Maybe after we go dancing, we could take a walk."

Whitney stilled. "On the pier?"

Cage smiled. This was easier than he thought it would be. "That's what I was thinking."

Without a word, she yanked her hand out of his and stood. She stormed toward the door. Cage called out to her, but the pain in his leg wouldn't let him keep up. Once outside, he found her standing by his car.

"I want to go home," she said and stared hard at the car.

Cage swallowed, not really sure what he'd done to fuck this up.

He placed a hand on her shoulder, but she jerked away from him.

"Whitney, what did I do?"

She turned around. Tears brimmed her beautiful eyes. "Take me home now, or I'm calling a cab."

Cage nodded, not really sure what else to do. At least if she was in his car, he'd have a chance of figuring it out.

CHAPTER TWELVE

CAGE TRIED TO START a conversation with Whitney several times, but each time he was shot down in the worse way possible: silence. Whatever he had done, Whitney was angrier than he'd ever seen her.

They stopped outside her house, and he turned to her.

"Please," he said quietly. "Tell me what I did. I just wanted us to have a fun date."

Whitney turned to face him. Anger radiated off of her.

"What? By using the same date that you use on every other tramp?" she spit out at him.

Cage paled. He'd thought he was giving her a good date. It was tested. It worked.

"It's not like that," he said quickly. "You don't understand."

Whitney gave a hollow laugh and opened the door.

"I'm sure it's not," she said and glared at him. "Except Candy filled me in. Thanks for the shitty beer."

She stomped out of the car and slammed the door.

Cage cursed his leg as he struggled to get out of the car and make his way up the stairs.

It couldn't end like this. He wasn't going to let it.

"Whitney," he called out, but she was already to the door.

His knee burned as he forced himself to half-jog up the stairs. She'd just unlocked the door as he climbed the last step.

"Wait," he said and quickly walked over to her.

He cursed the lack of railing on the side of her porch.

His knee shook, and he would have liked nothing more than to lean against something. Cage rested his hand against the house and turned so he could talk to her.

"What do you want, Cage?" she asked. Her voice was small and sounded tired.

He sighed. "Just give me a chance."

She furrowed her brow as she looked at him. "This was your chance."

"Look," he said and ran a hand through his hair, "I'm not good at this."

Whitney snorted. "Could have fooled me."

"It's not like that," he said and fumbled for the right words. "I didn't date before," he said and almost wished he hadn't said that from the look she was giving him. "I only know how to do it this one way."

He ran the hand in his hair along his neck.

"I just want to spend time with you," he said quietly. "However you'll let me."

Whitney stilled in the door. He didn't know if what he was saying meant anything, but he had to try.

"You are different from everyone," he said and stared into her beautiful green eyes. "You have to understand that."

Wind swept her hair in front of her face, and the soft lighting of the moon made her seem almost angelic. Cage swept the hair behind her ear and let his fingers linger on her face.

Whitney didn't even know where to go with him. He seemed so sweet and caring. There was a large part of her that hoped he meant what he said, but another part of her couldn't help but think he was just manipulating her.

She opened her mouth to say something but stopped when Cage suddenly turned and reached into the bush behind him.

Not understanding what was going on, Whitney pressed

herself against the door and watched as Cage struggled with whatever was in the bushes.

"Get your hands off me, pendejo," a younger voice said from the bush.

She gasped as Cage pulled out a boy who couldn't be more than twelve.

"Quit moving," Cage growled at the kid and pulled him into the light. "Fuck," he groaned. "You're Carlos's grandson."

* * *

Whitney still couldn't say she understood the whole thing. After they had managed to get the boy inside, they were surprised to find he and Hank were already friends. He sunk to his knees and laughed as Hank licked his happy face.

The boy was dirty all over and looked like he hadn't eaten a good meal in ages. It made her heart ache for him. Whatever had been going on with him was more than most adults could handle.

Whitney heated up some leftover meatloaf and potatoes. At first he glanced between Cage and Whitney warily, but the smell must have been too much for him to resist. She watched as he inhaled it and only hoped that he was chewing at least a little as he ate. When she offered to get a second plate, Cage frowned at her, but she ignored him. It had been a long night, and she could only guess that it was going to get longer.

This time she set out three plates. Cage opened his mouth to say something, but she glared at him.

"Nachos weren't much of a meal," she said.

His face paled a little at being called out, and although she knew she should feel bad, she didn't. She might forgive him, but that didn't mean she wasn't hungry.

They ate in silence, and when they were finished, the boy

picked up his plate and set it gently in the sink.

"I'm going to change," she said quietly to Cage. "Will you be okay?"

Cage frowned. "I can handle one punk kid."

She looked over to the boy, who now sat in the middle of her living room. Hank snuggled up on his lap.

"He's just a boy," she whispered.

Cage seemed to relax a little at her words. He limped over to the chair by the door in the living room and sank slowly into it. Despite his brave face, she could see his knee was hurting.

Whitney sighed and went into the kitchen. She pulled out a zip-top bag and placed some crushed ice inside. It wasn't the best, but it would do for now.

When she came back into the room, the boy and man were staring at one another.

She walked up to Cage and handed him the bag.

"Use it," she said and walked back to her bedroom.

She could hear him grunt in irritation and only hoped he didn't fight her on this. His ego was so fragile at times.

In her bedroom, she pulled off the black dress and tossed it onto the bed. She glared at it and the shoes she'd just kicked off. At least she wouldn't make that mistake again.

Whitney sighed and pulled a pair of black yoga pants from the drawer and a V-necked blue shirt. There was no reason to dress up now. She pulled her hair up into a pony tail and looked in the mirror. At least she was comfortable.

A little cleavage peeked out of the V, but there wasn't much to do about that.

She snorted to herself.

That amount of cleavage was nothing compared to Cage's other conquests. She was seeing a common theme with his women: big boobs and easy. She couldn't even begin to guess how she fit into that pattern.

Whitney sighed and made her way out of the room.

Whatever was going on between them was on hold until they figured out what the boy was doing. Everything in her said that he was harmless, and when it came to this sort of thing, she tended to trust her gut.

Cage was still in the chair, his leg raised up on the ottoman. She smiled a little when she saw the bag resting against his leg.

The boy sat on the floor, still with Hank. His eyes grew heavy and closed every once in a while.

Not bothering to ask, she got a blanket out of the closet and placed it over the boy.

He frowned up at her, and she saw the same stubborn streak she'd just seen in Cage. She might have laughed if he didn't look so pitiful.

"I don't need a blanket," he said and let it fall off his shoulder.

Hank sat up to see what was going on.

Whitney shrugged and sat on the couch.

"Well, it's for Hank," she said and placed her bare feet next to Cage's on the ottoman. "Unless you want him to be cold."

The boy looked down at Hank, who smiled and panted happily back at him. The chances of that dog getting cold were slim to none, but she didn't have a problem stretching the truth to get what she wanted.

She watched as the boy wrapped the blanket around himself and Hank.

"What's your name?" she asked when he was snuggled in.

The boy looked over to her and then Cage.

"Alex," he said.

She didn't push. There was no need. He had been seeking her out. He'd talk soon enough.

A knock came at the door, and Cage rose to answer it.

Alex tensed.

"It's Trent," he said to her.

Alex relaxed.

Cage came in and took a seat next to her. As much as she was irritated with him, she was glad to have him near her.

Trent took the seat Cage had just left. They sat silently just letting the situation sink in.

"You're the kid from the shop," Trent said finally.

"Alex is Carlos's grandson," Cage said.

Trent raised a brow.

"So, Alex," Trent said from an arm chair. "It was you leaving those things for Whitney?"

The boy looked over to Whitney and then down at Hank in his lap.

"She saved Hank," he said quietly. He said the name slowly, as if testing it out.

Whitney leaned forward. "Do you know how he was hurt?"

Alex looked up at her. Fear was in his eyes. He shook his head quickly.

Cage looked over to Trent, who was wearing the same hard expression he'd seen him wear when he didn't want to do something.

"Not telling us puts Whitney in danger," Trent said.

Whitney whipped around to glare at him, but Trent ignored her. Cage placed a hand on her leg, and when she looked at him, he nodded. His only hope was that she understood how serious this all was.

"Did the Los Malos put you up to this?" Cage asked.

He watched as Whitney's eyes widened with the realization of how deep things went.

Alex shook his head.

He believed him. The boy had been scared when the bell rang. Alex was in as much danger as the rest of them.

"We can't help you if you don't tell us something," Trent said and leaned back.

The boy continued to pet Hank in his lap.

"I just wanted to help," he said quietly. "Sometimes they bring them in. They are so scared, and I just didn't know what to do."

They listened silently as the boy spoke.

"They hate me," Alex said and rubbed his eyes on his shoulder. "They'd kill me, but some of the guys knew my papa and abuelo."

Cage cringed at the mention of Paco and Carlos. Both had lost their lives the day of the fire, the day he'd been shot. Only Carlos died with dignity, whereas Paco died by Ryder's hand when he was saving his woman. The kid had been through hell and was still living it even now.

"Who is the dog the chip and collar belonged to?" Whitney asked.

She leaned forward but hadn't thrown off his hand. Cage could only hope it was a good sign.

Alex shook his head and looked back down.

"Look," she said softly. "You wanted me to help. Well, you have to give me something here. I want to help you, Alex."

The boy looked up to her, and for the first time, Cage thought they might get somewhere with him.

"They keep the dogs," he said. "They come in with trucks, and a man takes out that metal thing in them."

Whitney looked to him with horror in her eyes.

"Where do they take the dogs?" Trent asked. He'd been quiet for some time, and Cage only assumed he was taking things in.

Alex shook his head. "I don't know," he said. "I'm not allowed to go. Like I said. They hate me, and they don't trust me."

Whitney cleared her throat. "And Hank?"

Alex swallowed. "He was strong, and he bit one of the men." He started to cry, and she got up to place an arm around him. "They kicked him. They were going to kill him."

"So you ran out with him," she said quietly.

Alex cried against her shoulder. "They beat me, but it was better than killing him."

Something snapped in Cage. More than anything in this world, he wanted to kill these men, to make sure they paid for what they had done to this boy.

Whitney smoothed down his hair and hugged the dirty boy.

"It's fine," she whispered. "We've got you now."

* * *

It took nearly an hour for the boy to calm down. He eventually fell asleep curled up on the floor with Hank.

Whitney brewed some coffee in the kitchen, where they were talking quietly.

"We should call the police," she said quietly.

Trent shook his head. "And tell them what? That they beat the boy and have stolen dogs, but we have no idea on the location? If the cops move now, they'll find nothing, and the Los Malos are just going to end up getting away with whatever else they are doing."

Whitney pursed her lips. "Alex will tell them."

Cage placed a hand on hers and squeezed. "How can he? This is a gang we're talking about. Do you know what happens to snitches?"

Her stomach churned. She didn't have to know for sure to have a pretty good guess. She'd seen the fear the boy had.

"Well," she said. She sighed and took a sip of her tea. "What do we do?"

Cage rubbed a finger across her hand, and she realized he still was holding her hand.

Part of her wanted to pull away, but after the child's story, she just couldn't.

The men grew quiet as they thought. She knew what had to be done. It was the only thing that was right in all this.

"He'll stay with me," she said.

Cage shook his head furiously.

"No fucking way," he said.

She pulled her hand back and crossed it over her chest.

"He needs a safe home, and that's just what I have," she said and eyed him.

"He does need a safe home," Trent said.

Cage looked between them, and she was fairly certain he was seeing things her way.

He sighed loudly.

"He'll come home with us," Cage said.

Whitney raised her brows in surprise.

"You?"

Cage frowned at her, and she knew that she'd hit a chord with him.

"He's a kid, not a baby. He'll be fine," he said and rubbed his eyes hard. "Besides, at least I'll know you're safe, and he will be as well. If the Los Malos go after him, I'd rather them run into Trent and me than you."

Her heart warmed at his honesty. He might be the worst person to plan a date, but Cage wasn't a bad man.

"It's settled then," Trent said and stood. "We take the boy."

With all the ease in the world, Trent went into the living room and scooped up the sleeping boy. It must have been ages since he slept so well. He didn't even stir at the movement.

She watched as Caged opened the door and then walked out to the car to open it as well. Trent slid Alex in the back of his car and then climbed into the driver seat. As Cage made his way back to her door, she watched as Trent drove off into the night.

"I'm sorry," Cage said when he reached the door.

She frowned a little.

"It was a shit date, and I'm a dick," he said.

It might not have been the most eloquent of speeches, but it touched her.

"I'll get this sorted out," he said and nodded in the direction Trent had drove. "Maybe you'll want to try again."

Whitney stayed silent as he walked slowly to his car and climbed in.

She didn't really know what to say. There were too many emotions warring within her.

He flashed his lights, and she knew he was waiting for her to go in.

Whitney walked inside and flicked the lock.

As she watched his lights trail off into the distance, she knew only one thing. Cage was a mystery to her, but that didn't have to be a bad thing.

CHAPTER THIRTEEN

JUST LIKE EVERY MORNING, the sun poured into the bedroom and made sleeping impossible for Cage. He frowned at the sound of laughter and the smell of food. Maybe he was still dreaming, and something weird was about to appear.

He blinked his eyes a few times as reality came back. The boy. Alex.

Despite the grogginess clouding his mind, he forced himself to get up and head to the bathroom. He figured a quick shower ought to do the trick.

Cage got the water as hot as he could stand. He'd found that with his knee, it was the hotter the better, especially when it was stiff.

He stepped under the spray and wondered what the hell he was going to do about the kid. Despite having nieces and nephews, Cage didn't have the slightest idea what to actually do on a day-to-day basis with a kid. He'd contacted Reed, and his brother agreed that the best move for the moment was to keep the kid close to him. He was, after all, the potential key to unlocking the secrets of the Los Malos.

Though the first thing would need to be a bath. That kid was dirty from head to foot. Cage figured he'd have to get some clothes for him as well. Alex certainly wouldn't fit into anything Cage had in his closet for a long time.

Cage climbed out of the shower and made his way back into the bedroom. He could still hear the boy in the living room, listening to cartoons or something like that. Despite the rocky start, it was good to hear him laugh. After what that kid had been through, what Cage had put him through by getting Carlos killed, Alex had it coming.

A lump formed in his throat as he thought of Carlos and what he might say. The old man loved his grandson. It would have pissed him off to no end how he was being treated. The Los Malos would pay for everything they'd done. It was just a matter of time.

Cage gripped the jeans he'd pulled from the closet and slapped them in the air to knock out wrinkles. He carefully slipped on the pants and pulled up the zipper. He stopped when something scratched at the door.

"What the—"

He opened the door, and Hank rushed in to lick his still damp toes.

Cage stared at the little dog, not quite sure what had happened. What was Hank doing at his place?

He made his way into the living room and was surprised to find a clean Alex dressed in different clothes.

"Hey," Alex said from the couch and went back to watching cartoons.

Something clattered in the kitchen near the back of the house.

Cage followed the sound of humming and running water.

When he reached the door, Cage leaned on the frame and stared in shock at Whitney doing dishes. She hummed happily, despite being somewhat off-key at times, and swayed her ass to the rhythm she'd created in her head.

"Hey, Alex," she said as she rinsed off her hands. "What do you say we make cupcakes la—"

Whitney froze. She'd been thinking about Cage all night, and now here he was. Shirtless. Sure, it was his place, but didn't the man own a damn shirt?

Despite herself, she followed the line of his chest until she reached the hair that dipped just below the underwear peeking out of his unbuttoned jeans.

"Shit," she whispered.

Cage grinned at her. She'd come to surprise him, and he still managed to get the upper hand.

He slowly moved into the small kitchen.

"I like chocolate," he said and placed his hands on either side of the sink, effectively blocking her in.

"Chocolate." She swallowed and let out the breath she'd been holding.

"Morning, Whitney," he said quietly. His low voice made her nipples stand up and beg for attention.

"Morning," she whispered back.

"I'm surprised to see you here," he said and leaned back. She watched as he made his way to the table in the kitchen and sat down.

She took in deep breaths. Now that he wasn't so close, she found it was easier. She silently cursed her treacherous body and Cage.

"I came to make breakfast and make sure Alex was taken care of," she said and went back to wiping off the counter. "I wasn't sure if you'd be able to handle a kid."

Despite herself, she was surprised to find the place so clean. Most men were at least a little messy. Maybe living with a SEAL had something to do with it.

Cage grabbed a piece of bacon off the plate on the table and munched on it as he watched her.

"Where's Trent?" he asked.

Whitney shrugged. "He let me in this morning and said the house was in my hands."

"Very capable hands I'd say." Cage grinned.

She frowned. He was toying with her. She needed to at least reestablish a little bit of control given how her body was reacting.

"I could go if—" she began.

Cage jumped up to block her way. "Don't go," he said.

"Please don't go."

She smiled and stepped a little closer. Maybe he needed to know that he wasn't the only one that could be cocky, even in his own home.

"Good," she said and leaned down. Her shirt dipped a little, and her face burned as he glanced at her breasts. "Trent is going to be back later to watch Alex during our date."

Cage frowned. "Date?"

Whitney poked him in the chest and sat up. "You owe me a real date with the real Cage, not the standard Cage Seduction Package."

She could see the confusion on his face, but that was fine with her. She'd much rather have that than the slick guy from last night. When she'd fully digested the night, she understood, but the whole thing still irked her a bit.

"What about my cupcakes?" Alex said from the door.

Whitney grinned at the boy. "Why do you think we're making the cupcakes?"

Alex grinned back and whooped his way back to the living room.

"About those cupcakes…" Cage frowned and stared at her. "I still get to have some, right?"

Whitney laughed at his expression and patted him on the shoulder.

"We'll have them tonight. You help make them, you help eat them," she said and went back to cleaning.

She jumped when his arms wrapped around her middle. His warm chest pressed against her.

"Thank you," he whispered. "I won't blow it this time."

She shivered when he walked away and turned to look where he had been. For her sake, she hoped he was right.

* * *

Whitney smiled as she watched Alex eat his cupcake. He'd

already practically inhaled the first one and was savoring the second, resulting in a chocolate mess around his mouth. It was amazing to her how messy a kid could be.

"That was amazing," Cage said and leaned back in the chair next to her.

She looked over to him and laughed.

"You got a little something on you," she said and pointed to the corner of his mouth.

Cage stuck out his tongue and tried to lick it off, but kept missing.

"Good?" he asked.

She snorted and leaned over him. She lightly swiped her finger over the spot.

"There," she said.

His hand reached out and grasped her wrist. Finger still pointed out, Cage brought the frosted digit to his mouth and sucked off the frosting.

"My chocolate," he said to her.

Something fluttered deep inside Whitney as he stared at her.

"Gross," Alex said and wrinkled his nose. "Old people are gross."

Cage frowned at the boy. "Who you calling old?"

"I think he was calling you old, and I'm apt to agree."

Trent grinned from the door of the kitchen.

Whitney laughed at the playful banter. It was nice to finally be able to completely relax, even if for only a few minutes.

"So I hear I'm watching you tonight," Trent said to the boy.

Alex nodded and swallowed the last bite of his cupcake.

"What do you say we see how many of these we can eat before we puke?"

The boy's face lit up, and he nodded.

"No," Whitney said and glared at the two of them. "At least eat some real food first."

Trent rolled his eyes dramatically and then winked to Alex. "Fine. We'll eat."

She sighed and stood from the table. A part of her was almost sad for their time with Alex to end. But still, she wanted to know more. About Cage, about his knee, but mostly, what was going to happen with them.

Whitney looked over to Cage, who had been watching her quite a bit today.

"I just need a few minutes, and I'll be ready," she said with a smile.

Cage looked from his own t-shirt and jeans to her similar attire.

"Like this?" he asked.

She smiled at him and nodded. "Nothing fancy, just us."

"Gross," Trent said, wrinkling his nose. "Get out of here before I'm sick."

Whitney chuckled as she made her way to the bathroom. She liked that Trent had brought himself to Alex's level. The boy needed someone he felt comfortable with. They were just getting to that with him, and she hated to see him retreat within himself again. From what she could tell, he'd been through a lot, even ignoring the violent deaths of his relatives.

She stepped in the bathroom and looked in the mirror. Well, her current outfit was about as casual as it got. Everything in her hoped that this would work, that she would know the real Cage at the end. She was taking a big risk, and she hoped it was worth it.

Despite her thoughts, she still pulled out the travel toothbrush. She might want to know him better, but that didn't mean that she didn't want more. He lit a fire in her, and she hoped to learn more about that as well. There was no reason she couldn't have the best of both worlds.

CHAPTER FOURTEEN

CAGE SAT NERVOUSLY across from Whitney in the little Italian bistro. It was quiet, cute and way too personal. Not that he had anything to hide, but still, there was no room for error. He felt so close to the edge with her, and he didn't want to screw up something that felt like a chance for true happiness.

"Cage?" she said and gave him a warm smile.

He looked to his right and found the waiter staring back at him.

"I ordered a glass of wine, but they have beer as well," she said.

Cage let out a sigh of relief. It wasn't that he hated wine, but it wasn't his favorite. He certainly was far from an expert on the best wines.

"That sounds good," he said.

The man nodded and walked away.

"Thanks," he said, smiling at her.

He felt silly not really knowing what to do. For all the dangerous situations he'd been in, he felt more out of his element in the small restaurant.

"I thought this would be a good choice," she said and looked around. "Quiet but not fancy. They have wine but also beer. Plus it's family style."

Cage nodded and looked around. Now that she said all that, he could see that it really was a good pick. It had something that each of them would like. This wasn't about her forcing her tastes on him. She was trying to compromise, so they could both be happy.

"How did you find this place? Come here with another date?"

He frowned, thinking that maybe Ted had taken her there. He didn't hate the guy, but he didn't want to be in any man's shadow.

"You mean Ted?"

He shrugged. Might as well get it out in the open.

"You have to understand," she said and let out a quiet sigh. "I never dated Ted," she said. "Actually, I never dated much of anyone."

He wanted to feel happy that she hadn't been there with another man, that this spot was special for both of them. Instead, he just felt bad that he'd asked.

"Lisa," she said. "She's always trying new places. She's been all over the world and is constantly trying to get me out of my comfort zone. Sometimes she even succeeds."

Cage smiled at her. He liked the way she talked about her friends. It was like he talked about his family.

"I've never really dated much either," he said.

Whitney nearly choked on the water she was drinking.

"That's a little hard to believe," she said.

Cage laughed a little. It likely was hard to believe. "Look, we both know my past, but I wouldn't really call that dating. It was something, I don't know what exactly, but not dating."

He stared at her from across the table, letting all the desire he felt pour through him to her.

The waiter came back and set a glass of wine in front of her and some imported beer in front of him.

He took a drink off the bottle and set it down, somewhat surprised. It wasn't half bad.

"So we both suck at dating," Whitney said. She laughed and took a drink of her wine.

He liked it much better when she was laughing.

"I wouldn't say we suck at it," he said. "Maybe we just

weren't dating the right people."

Whitney swallowed hard. She didn't even know where to go when he said things like that. A part of her wanted to believe that it was just a line, but she knew, deep down, that Cage didn't need to use lines. He was sincere with what he said. That sincerity both impressed and terrified her. That kind of sincerity led to real emotional risks.

She was thankful when the large bowl of spaghetti and meatballs arrived at the table.

When he nodded for her to hold up her plate for him to serve her, she could feel the blush spread over her face.

He was funny and sweet, someone she wanted to get to know better. They finished their meal talking mostly about their jobs. His scared the crap out of her, but still, it was honest, and, in many cases, helped other people. She couldn't really fault that.

At the end of the meal, he grabbed the ticket before she could even offer.

She understood with him. So much of what he did was about being the big man.

As they left the bistro, she smiled warmly at him. The date had been nice.

"How about a gelato?" she said.

Cage frowned. "I'm not sure."

She pointed through the park across the street to a stand.

"It's like the best sort of ice cream you've ever had."

"Oh. That's what it is?" His eyes lit up at the idea of ice cream.

He took a step, and she noticed that he was straining more than she'd previously seen.

"Can you make it?" she asked.

Cage stiffened beside her.

"I'm great," he said and struggled to now take steps without shaking.

"Stop," Whitney said so forcefully that Cage came to a complete halt.

He stared at her, waiting.

"I want Cage," she said. "The Cage from now. Not Cage from two months ago, who had no problem picking up any woman and going home with her. I want the man that has been through things. The one that bears the proof of that. I don't need you to pretend for me, Cage."

He looked away, and she watched him. His throat bobbed as he swallowed hard.

"I can make it," he said and looked back to her. "If we go slow."

She nodded. All she wanted, no, all she needed was honesty.

They slowly made their way across the street and into the park. They found a bench not far in, and she insisted he sit and save their seats.

She hurried over and picked up pistachio and chocolate gelatos.

When she came back, Whitney sat next to him on the bench and stared out across the park.

"I know what you were doing there," he said and took a bite of his chocolate.

Whitney looked over to him and frowned. "Getting you back for dinner?"

Cage raised a brow and took another bite.

Whitney took a bite of her own before saying anything else.

"So I care," she said and placed a hand on his sore leg. The muscles under her hand twitched, and she knew he wanted to move away. "If you don't take care of it, you'll permanently damage it."

Cage sighed. "Everyone seems to know what's best for me."

Whitney snorted. "I might not be a human doctor, but I

know a bit about anatomy." She stared hard at him. "I don't want you to hurt yourself over gelato."

He stared back at her and finally nodded.

Her eyes now fixed on her gelato. "You said before the shooting had something to do with Carlos."

Cage cleared his throat, and she looked up at him. He was staring off in the distance.

"I was shot while on assignment," he said. "It's what took out my knee. The shooters were obviously trying to cripple me."

She gasped.

"It was Carlos, Alex's grandfather, who saved me. He just jumped in front and took the bullet." His voice was distant, and she could tell that he thought often about the incident.

"How sad," she said.

"The thing with Alex, that's what's sad. Carlos and I are men. We made our choices. He's just a damn kid. If Carlos had been alive, none of that crap would have happened to him."

Whitney shook her head. "You don't know that."

Cage sighed and leaned his head back to look between the branches at the sky above them.

"Maybe," he said. "But I will take down these bastards. What they did to that kid…"

His voice wavered, and she laced her fingers with his. She understood. She'd been feeling the same way. The men of Los Malos were monsters. They had tried to break the spirit of a boy, and it burned her up inside.

"He's safe," she whispered. "We'll keep him that way."

Cage squeezed her hand.

She breathed in deeply and waited for him to move closer, to close the distance between them. Cage stood.

"Speaking of," he said and nodded to the car. "We should get back before he gets to bed."

Slightly disappointed, she stood. He was right though.

Alex needed to be surrounded by people who cared about him.

With her fingers still laced with his, they made their way back. The date had gone well. Now she only hoped they would get the chance for more dates.

* * *

Cage cursed himself in his head the whole ride home. It was the perfect moment to kiss her, and he'd blown it.

He hadn't been wrong. They did need to get back, but he could have spared a few minutes.

When they stopped outside the house, he frowned at the darkness inside. He'd given up a kiss to get back early, and they were already both asleep?

He jumped at the sound of his phone. When he pulled it out, he looked at the screen.

TRENT

"Yeah," he said, answering the phone.

"We're at your mom's," Trent said before Cage could even ask.

"What?"

"Before you start getting pissed, we were bribed with fried chicken and pie," Trent said over the phone. "We both were still hungry."

He could hear Alex in the background laughing, and despite the irritation he felt, his mother was a woman with more than enough love to share.

"When are you going to be home?" he asked and glanced over to Whitney, who seemed interested in the conversation.

"See that's the thing, now she's pulled out movies and started on cake," Trent said eagerly.

"How late?" he asked.

"We'll just stay here and meet up with you at the office," Trent said.

Cage laughed loudly into the phone. "What's she offering for breakfast?"

"Home-fucking-made cinnamon rolls," Trent said excitedly but stopped for a moment. "Sorry, ma'am."

Cage snorted and turned to Whitney. "Well, enjoy your home-fucking-made cinnamon roll, traitor."

Whitney gave him a lopsided smile. He loved the look.

"Dog might need to go out when you get home," Trent said. "Gotta go. Cake."

The line went silent.

"We've been traded for cake, fried chicken and homemade cinnamon rolls," Cage grinned.

Whitney opened her door and grinned back at him.

"I'd trade us for that as well," she said with a laugh.

"Hank is still here," he said and made his way out of the car.

He slowly walked up the sidewalk. The last few days had taken a toll on his leg, and he was done hiding. Whitney understood, and he didn't have to pretend with her.

Cage opened the door and cursed as Hank zipped out into the lawn.

The dog found the nearest flower and proceeded to water it.

"Men," Whitney groaned and walked to the lawn to get him after his business.

When she came back up the steps, her face was hidden slightly by the shadows.

It was killing him. Should he go in for the kiss or just thank her for a nice evening? The last thing he wanted to do was fuck it up again.

Instead, Whitney made the move for both of them.

"Aren't you going to invite me in?" she asked.

CHAPTER FIFTEEN

WHITNEY MOVED IN A LITTLE CLOSER. The scent of Cage's aftershave floated through the air. It was driving her crazy.

"I didn't get a tour earlier," she said as she stepped in, her voice low and husky.

She set Hank on the floor after shutting the door and found Cage standing close behind her.

Whitney backed up until she was flush against the door.

He stepped closer, and she gasped when his hard body pushed against her own.

"Tell me I'm not reading this wrong," he said. His voice shook with uncertainty.

Her hands slipped under the soft t-shirt he was wearing. He groaned as she worked her fingers along the hard muscles there.

"Fuck, Whitney," he hissed and glared at her. "Tell me."

Whitney leaned forward and ran her lips over his, taunting him.

"I want…" she said against his mouth. "I want you to show me your room."

She stared at him through her lashes and waited for what seemed like forever.

Cage pressed hard against her, his body a solid wall as his mouth plundered her own.

Whitney pulled her hands from his shirt and wrapped them around his neck and in his hair.

His hard ridge pressed just above the spot she wanted it most.

His hand wrapped around her leg and lifted it up. With the new angle, he pressed hard against her aching clit.

"Shit," he cursed. He was shaking.

With more force than she knew she could manage, Whitney pushed him back. Cage sighed loudly, and she knew he was misunderstanding.

"Come with me," she said and started walking toward his bedroom.

Cage paused for a moment, and she didn't know if he was trying to convince himself she didn't want him or he didn't want her. Without a thought, she pulled off the t-shirt she was wearing and tossed it on the ground.

His breathing picked up, but at least his feet were moving. Whitney didn't stop. She unsnapped her pants and slid them down her legs when she reached his room.

Cage stood in the door, staring at her. She started to wonder if maybe she didn't measure up. She wasn't really all that big breasted, and she'd never really been thought of as curvy.

"Beautiful," he whispered.

His sweet whisper lanced through her and shook her to the core.

She slowly made her way to him. Once again, her hands slipped under his shirt, but this time she had only one purpose.

It slid easily over his head, and she tossed it over her shoulder. She kept her eyes on him. The glow from the light outside was just enough.

She kissed her way down his chest. The light dusting of hair excited her, especially the closer she got to the snap on his pants.

Whitney dropped to her knees as she continued her kisses. She slowly pulled the zipper down and found his hard cock tenting his underwear.

His pants fell to the floor, and she smiled at the thought he was letting her undress him.

One hand made its way around to his ass. She loved the feel of the hard muscles there.

Whitney ran her hands up and down his legs. The closer she got to his tip, the more he shook. Instead of giving him what he wanted, Whitney kissed and nipped the flesh on his thighs before dipping lower and lower to his damaged leg.

"Whitney," he said and pulled back.

She shook it off and stood in front of him.

"Take me to bed, Cage," she whispered.

He groaned and stepped out of his pants. Whitney moved away and climbed onto the bed.

Cage stepped toward her. If he didn't pace himself, he'd never make it through.

"Cage," she sighed and tossed her bra to him.

"Fuck it," he grunted.

Cage made his way onto the bed and sighed when she climbed on top of him. Her wet center pressed hard against his throbbing dick.

"Shit," he said.

Whitney moved hard against him. Her little breaths were driving him crazy.

Cage moved his hands up her body and wrapped them around her breasts. Her nipples pressed hard against his hand.

In one move he had her pressed against him, his hot mouth lapping at her peaks.

"Oh," she whispered when his teeth nibbled her.

She moved faster over him, rubbing her wet center against his still clothed cock.

Whitney grunted in frustration.

"Cage," she said.

"Shhh," he said and found the edge of her panties. "I got you, baby."

In one quick move, he whipped off her panties. He moaned when her hand slipped into his underwear and stroked him.

"Now, Cage," she moaned and pulled hard on his underwear.

Breasts forgotten, Cage struggled to pull down the one thing he'd give anything to rid himself of at that moment.

With his good leg, he pushed his underwear down and kicked them off.

Cage felt wet pussy slip over him.

"Whitney," he groaned. "I don't—"

His words were cut off as she pushed down hard against him and buried him deep inside her.

Whitney took in deep breaths as she adjusted to his size. Rough fingers found her clit and circled the hard bead. The harder he circled, the more she started to ache.

"Shit, honey, if you don't quit squeezing me like that, I'm never going to make it," Cage said. His breathing came hard, and sweat already coated his chest.

She ran her hands along his chest and down his arms to where his hands were.

Just like earlier, she laced her hands with his.

She slid, slowing pulling out everything but the head. Each time she slid back down, his cock slid more smoothly into her.

Cage worked at her clit, pressing hard and urging her on more.

She bounced on him, grinding him deeper and deeper into her.

His fingers held on to her breasts but never squeezed too hard.

She let go of his hands and leaned back a bit, the new position pushing him hard into her cervix.

Cage cursed, and she sat up.

"Am I hurting you?" she said. She stilled with him deep inside her.

"Fuck no," he grunted and pulled her hard against him.

She gasped when he surged up into her. His hips buckled wildly as he held her firmly against him.

"Cage," she moaned his name over and over, unable to even think as his coarse hairs rubbed against her aching clit.

"Whitney," he moaned.

She could feel him swell inside her and felt her own release hit as she squeezed him hard. His hot cum sprayed deep inside her.

His hips stilled as they both rode through their orgasms.

She kissed his chest and traced her name through his hair there.

He smiled at her.

"You are so beautiful," he whispered.

She had never had someone say something like that to her. She wasn't the person men said were beautiful.

Whitney pulled herself up his body and placed a tender kiss on his lips.

"Good night, Cage." She yawned and slipped off his body. He stretched out his arm where she laid her head and snuggled next to him.

Sleep came easily for once. All she needed was him.

* * *

Cage woke up feeling far more excited than he had the past few mornings. The sun still peeked through the window, but unlike the last few days, he didn't really care if it was a dream. He wasn't moving.

The mouth moving over his dick hummed a little, and his eyes shot open.

"Whitney?" he asked between breaths.

He watched as she released his dick to smile up at him. It was far more erotic than he would have ever thought.

"Morning," she said.

Her naked form sat nestled between his legs, and he watched as she ran her tongue along the side of his dick and then down the other side. Her slick tongue left a wet trail.

She gripped him in her hand as she began to kiss all around him, running her devilish tongue along his tight balls.

"Shit," he said and tensed as she sucked on them.

He watched as a little precum slipped from his tip, and she swiped her tongue along the slit.

She still didn't put her mouth back on him and pull him in as she had before.

Whitney went back to kissing and nibbling the flesh around. She sank lower and lower. His mind was having trouble concentrating with the spiral she'd decided to add to her hand job.

Cage jumped when her mouth touched the tender scars on his knee.

"Whitney," he said and tried to move away.

She placed a hand on his thigh and stared up at him.

"All of you, Cage," she said.

He knew what she meant. She wanted all of him.

He leaned his head back on the pillow and waited as she placed gentle kisses on his knee. Cage didn't need to watch her as she stared at his jagged scars, as she came face to face with the destruction that was left from his once-shattered knee.

"Cage," she whispered.

He opened an eye and looked down at her.

"It's a part of you," she whispered. "And there isn't one part of you that I don't like."

His heart ached at her words. It was everything that he'd longed to hear.

Cage reached down and pulled her up the bed. Whitney positioned herself over him and leaned down to kiss him as he pressed deep into her.

Cage grunted at the position. It wasn't going to work. He

needed more.

Whitney gasped as she flipped in the air and landed on her back.

She opened her mouth to ask if the position was going to be okay but moaned loudly as he pushed into her.

Cage found her mouth and kissed her as he worked himself in and out with all his might.

She moaned against him and wrapped her legs around his back.

He broke away from the kiss and pressed in deeper.

Her body shook as he moved in her faster and harder than even the previous night.

Whitney could feel her insides start to clench.

"Not yet," he whispered harshly in her ear.

She nodded and tried to keep her body from doing the one thing it burned to do.

Cage slipped his hands up her back to pull himself in harder.

The sound of their wet slapping filled the room and only added to her need to come.

"Cage," she hissed and scrapped her nails along his back.

"Almost," he whispered.

The bed shook with each thrust, rocking hard against the wall.

With one hard thrust, Cage shouted to her.

"Now!"

She shuddered hard around him as he flexed inside her.

Spent, he collapsed on her, breathing hard against her neck.

"I hope to wake up like this every morning," he rumbled in her ear.

Whitney laughed and wrapped her arms around him.

"Only if you make me breakfast." She grinned.

Cage sat up slightly and stared at her through half-open

eyes.

"What sort of breakfast?"

Whitney nibbled her lip. "Home-fucking-made cinnamon rolls."

Cage laughed and rolled her until she was on top. His cock was still hard inside her.

She stared down at him in surprise. "How about just the fucking part?" he asked and surged up into her.

Whitney groaned and leaned over.

"Any time you want," she whispered.

CHAPTER SIXTEEN

WHITNEY COULDN'T STOP SMILING. She knew she shouldn't be this happy, but she was. Cage had made her the happiest she'd ever been.

She watched him as he slowly made his way up the stairs at his office. He stopped and looked back at her questioningly.

A blush spread across her face at being caught.

"Later," he growled at her.

She caught up with him on the steps and slipped her hand into his.

Cage laced his fingers with hers, and she smiled at the sweet gesture.

"I'm never going to make it to the top if you keep staring at my ass like that," he whispered.

She looked over to him and then back to the top of the stairs.

"I have no idea what you're talking about," she said quietly.

He let go of her hand. Moments later, his hand was resting firmly on her ass.

"You aren't the only one who'd like to stare," he said in her ear.

"Cage Allen," said a shrill voice cutting through the air. "You let that poor woman walk up the stairs without accosting her."

"Fuck," he mumbled but dropped his hand back to his side. They laced fingers once again.

Whitney looked around and found an older woman at the door to an office. She waved excitedly to her. Whitney managed a small smile and waved back.

"What the hell is all this about?" she whispered to him.

"That's my mom," he said with a grimace.

When they made it to the top of the stairs, the older woman smiled warmly at her.

"Oh, Whitney," she said and pulled her in for a hug. "I've heard so much about you."

Whitney let go of Cage to pat the older woman on the back.

"You too," she said politely.

The woman pulled back and laughed. Her curly salt and pepper hair bounced as she did.

"Oh, now, I know my son," she said and looked over to Cage. "The last thing he wants to do is bring a woman home to meet his mother."

"Ma," Cage said and looked away, his face reddening.

"Marilyn," the older woman said and smiled at Whitney. "I can't tell you how happy I am."

"Mother," Cage ground out and laced his fingers through Whitney's again. "You're going to scare her off."

Marilyn frowned at her son and turned to Whitney. "Am I scaring you?"

Whitney held back the laugh threatening to burst out.

"No," she said.

Cage sighed. "You shouldn't encourage her," he whispered.

Marilyn glared at him.

"Where's the kid?" he asked.

Marilyn grinned from ear to ear.

"Oh, I like Alex," she said and made her way down the hall. "He calls me ma'am and does dishes. He also eats everything I set in front of him." She turned to look at Cage, anger there for the first time. "Whoever had him wasn't feeding him. That boy is underweight, and macaroni isn't going to cut it."

Cage squeezed Whitney's hand, and as much as she wanted to agree, she knew it was hard for him to hear that he might not be providing like he wanted.

"Maybe we should go grocery shopping today," Whitney said with a smile.

Cage grimaced, and she wondered if she'd said something wrong.

"Cage," Marilyn said. "You mean you didn't invite her to the family dinner?"

Whitney blanched at the idea of a family dinner. It sounded intimate. And emotionally dangerous.

"I was planning on asking her when the time was right," he said through gritted teeth.

Marilyn huffed and rolled her eyes. "Well, looks like that time is now. I'll just give you a moment."

She stepped inside a room where Trent and Alex were sitting. Both had cookies stuffed into their mouths.

Cage pulled her into the next room and shut the door.

She watched as he paced back and forth, running a hand through his hair.

"Family is important to us," he said. "It can be really great, but there are times when it can also be really annoying."

"Like now?" she offered.

Cage nodded. Her stomach twisted.

"Look, if you don't want me there…" she started.

"No," Cage said quickly and stepped in front of her. His breath blew across her face. "I want you there more than anything," he said quietly. "I just don't want to rush you. I'm so afraid that I'm going to screw this up, and you'll run from me."

She placed her hands against his cheeks and pressed a gentle kiss to his lips.

"You won't mess this up," she said quietly. "I told you. I

just want the real Cage. As long as that's the guy I get, then we're good."

He stared down at her, and she wondered what he saw when he looked at her. Whatever it was made her heart ache to hold him.

"Whitney," he said, smiling at her, "will you go to dinner at my parents?"

She giggled a little at the almost teen-like question.

"Yes," she said and kissed him again on the lips.

His hand slipped down her back, and he groaned.

"Maybe we should make dinner short tonight," he said.

"You better not, Cage," his mother shouted from the other room.

He sighed loudly. "Quit listening, Ma," he shouted back.

She opened the door next to them and glared at him.

"Be good, or I won't make cornbread."

Cage pressed his lips together but didn't say anything else.

"I'm so glad you're coming, dear." Marilyn beamed at Whitney. "Is there anything you need?"

Whitney looked over to Cage and then back to his mother. She took a few steps toward her.

"Got any embarrassing baby photos?"

Cage grunted loudly.

"Oh, I like this one," Marilyn said. "She's going to fit in nicely."

* * *

After a few minutes of chatting, Cage ushered Whitney and Alex down the stairs while his mother was still preoccupied with Trent and his lack of facial care.

"Move it," Cage said and made it across the room in record time.

Whitney laughed as they made it outside.

"She's totally awesome," she said.

Cage rolled his eyes. "You mean she's totally meddle-some."

Alex shrugged. "I like her," he said. "She gave me pie and cake in the same night."

Cage snorted. "That's just how she ropes you in."

He stopped when the boy paled and gripped his arm with more strength than he thought possible.

Cage followed his line of sight and frowned.

Roberto stood across the street from them, leaning against his car.

"So this is where you been, you little piece of shit?" Roberto shouted from across the way. He spit on the ground.

Whitney wrapped her arms around the boy to stop his shaking.

"*Me traicionaste! Te quiero muerto*," Roberto said. One of his men stepped out of the car.

Cage didn't know a lot of Spanish, but pretty much everyone knew that muerto meant death.

The associate slid a finger across his throat and then stepped into the car.

"You're brave now, but you won't always have your gimp friend around," Roberto said. "How's the knee, puta?"

Cage snorted, his hand dropping to his jacket holster. "Why don't you come over here and find out?"

"Oh, I will soon enough." He grinned and got back into the car with his friend.

Cage watched as the men rolled away. His hand still rested on his gun.

Whitney hugged Alex as he continued to shake.

"They don't mean it," he said quickly. "It's a threat. To make sure you don't talk."

Alex shook his head and stared up at Cage. "You know they mean it."

Cage watched the road for a moment before shaking his head.

"Well, you know what? Fuck them," Cage said. He frowned. "They come near you, they're going to have to deal with me and my family. The Los Malos are a bunch of punks. A few Allens could take them on before, and that's when we weren't watching their asses and ready for their crap."

Alex's eyes grew into saucers.

"Why would you do this?" he whispered.

The question struck him and made Cage hurt inside.

"Because that's what family does," he said. "Now get in the car. We're got to buy food for my house before my mother brings in the National Guard."

Alex smiled at him and climbed in. He watched Whitney as she slipped into the front. The fear that was there only made him love her more.

Cage froze. Love?

The idea hadn't even really sunk in that he might, although he'd been thinking about her nearly every day for the last five months. It did make sense.

Cage shook his head. He didn't have time to sort out his feelings when there was roast beef he could be buying. The Los Malos weren't going to come after them at the grocery store.

CHAPTER SEVENTEEN

WHITNEY TOOK IN DEEP BREATHS as she walked with Cage and Alex up to a house with about a million cars parked outside.

She glanced over to Cage, who seemed to be taking it all easily enough. Even if it was his parents' house, she still thought he'd be a bit more nervous.

"Relax," he whispered. "It will be fine."

She swallowed and kept walking. Before they had even stepped onto the porch, Marilyn was outside with an older man who bore more than a passing resemblance to Cage, except with green eyes.

"Kids are out back, Alex," she said and smiled warmly at him.

The boy had been very quiet since the incident outside the office, and Whitney only hoped that he wasn't focusing too much on it. They would keep him safe. From the looks of the cars, the entire Allen clan was gathered, probably more than enough burly men and tough women to protect one boy.

"Come on in," Marilyn said. She then turned to the man standing behind her. "This is my husband, James."

Whitney took his hand and stared openly at the man. It was just remarkable how much his children looked like him.

"I know," Marilyn said and let out a harrumph. "They took after him."

James kissed her cheek, and she softened a little. "There can only be one you in this house."

Whitney smiled and turned to Cage, who was shaking his

head.

"All right, get a room you two," he said and grinned.

Whitney looked around the room. The whole house was packed with people, mostly men she'd noticed at Cage's office.

"Are all of these people your family?" she whispered to him.

Cage laughed a little. "Might as well be," he said and nodded to a few. "Some are cousins and family friends. Others are people we've adopted along the way."

She marveled at the number of people.

Her mom was always moving on to the next husband or boyfriend, so it didn't really matter who the other family was, and her dad didn't care to stick around long enough to even think about marriage.

Really, it was just the three of them and never all in the same room. The only time she could really see that happening was at her wedding and that was if they could pull themselves away from their own drama long enough to be concerned with hers. She didn't hate her parents, but when you don't spend the time to build ties, there is nothing there in the end.

They moved from room to room as Marilyn introduced her to brothers, cousins and friends. The names started to blur together. Finally, Whitney came across someone she knew.

"Oh, so bro finally nailed the vet," Meg said.

The spunky little woman was a force to be reckoned with.

"What the fuck, Meg!" Cage said with a glare.

"Cage!" his mother shouted from the other room.

He continued to glare at Meg until Whitney slipped her hand back into his.

She leaned forward slightly. "Who's to say I didn't nail him?" She winked.

Meg grinned from ear to ear. Whitney didn't really know what had gotten into her, but she nearly laughed when she turned to find Cage staring at her open-mouthed.

"He needs someone to keep him on his toes," Meg said. "He thinks he's big shit most of the time."

"How is it she hears me when I say fuck but not when you say shit?" Cage grumbled.

"Your voice carries, you idiot," his mother shouted from the other room.

Meg rolled her eyes at her brother. "Why don't you come meet the girls?"

She turned to Cage, who was staring warily at his sister.

"Don't get her into any trouble, or I'll sic Mom on you," he said.

Meg snorted. "Yeah? What can she do?"

"Well," her mother said from over her shoulder. "I could make sure that I have some little things for Liam to do when he's off work."

Marilyn smiled sweetly at her daughter.

Meg narrowed her eyes.

They all looked at Whitney in surprise when she burst out laughing.

"I think maybe one of your children took after you," Whitney said and whipped a tear from the corner of her eye.

"Yep," Marilyn said. "She'll fit in just fine."

Cage watched as his mother and sister pulled Whitney through the house to where the other women were gathered. He couldn't help but smile. Things were finally fitting into place.

He turned to scan the room for Trent, but movement outside caught his eye. Alex walked alone down the path to the dock.

As Cage made his way outside, he thought about the incident earlier with Roberto. He'd told the kid that nothing would happen, but he couldn't be sure of that. The only way that the Los Malos would stop was if someone like him gave them a reason to stop. Alex wasn't stupid. He knew this.

The land sloped down a bit before leading to the boat dock. Cage followed the wooden plank-covered path to the storage shed and dock.

Alex sat at the edge of the water and stared out across the way. He tossed rocks into the water absentmindedly.

"Won't catch any fish that way," Cage said as he got closer.

Alex stared up at him, his face somber.

He shrugged and went back to throwing the rocks.

Slowly, Cage lowered himself down. His knee ached a little but not as much as it likely should considering the previous night's activity.

"What's going on?" he asked.

Alex shrugged. "Nothing."

Cage stared at the kid. He had been so happy earlier, and those bastards had to take that from him.

He nudged the boy. "Spill it," he said. "I know those dicks from before are bothering you."

Alex stopped throwing rocks and looked over at him.

"Whitney doesn't like it when you curse around me," he said.

Cage shrugged. "I'm just calling it like I see it."

He stared at the boy and only hoped that he could see the sincerity in his face. If things were going to work, they were going to have to trust one another.

"They will come for me," Alex said. "Especially now that they know I'm been talking with the Allens."

Cage nodded. "Maybe," he said.

Alex's eyes went wide with fright.

"That's what I'm here for though," Cage said. "Not just me, everyone at the firm."

Tears pooled in the boy's eyes. Cage placed an arm around him, but he moved away quickly.

"What happens when you aren't around?" Alex said and

stood. "What happens when you don't want me anymore?"

Cage struggled to stand. Sitting was the easy part in all this.

By the time Cage finally made it to his feet, Alex was looking back out over the calm water. Occasionally he would wipe his face roughly against his shirt.

"I want you to listen to me," Cage said and forced the boy to look him in the eye. "Have I ever fed you a line of bull-shit?"

Alex shook his head, tears still in his eyes.

"So when I tell you that you can stay with me as long as you want, do you believe me?"

Alex hesitated for a moment and then shook his head.

"You grandfather gave his life for me," Cage said. A lump formed in the back of his throat. "I never knew why, but now I do. You will always have a place in my home and with my family. That's what we do here. Take in people who want a family and protect one another. That's why we're in the business we're in."

The sobs the boy had been holding in burst out. Alex threw himself hard against Cage and wrapped his arms around him.

"We are family," he whispered to Alex. "We take care of each other."

He placed a hand on his back and patted the boy until his tears had dried.

"Better?" he asked.

Alex let go and took in a shaky breath.

"Yeah."

"Good." He smiled at him. "Now let's go see if we can steal a piece of cake before my mom finds out."

"Busted," his mother called from the end of the dock.

They turned to find Whitney and his mother standing together.

"Alex, you come with me," Marilyn said.

She smiled at him warmly, and Cage knew she had over-heard their conversation. "I've got a big piece of cake with your name on it."

Cage frowned. "What about me?"

She glared at him but with far less anger than usual. "I don't give cake to men who teach children to steal."

Alex laughed and followed Marilyn inside. Cage's heart was lighter hearing the boy's laughter.

Whitney moved along the dock to where Cage stood. Everything he said made her so glad to know him. This was the real Cage, and there was nothing about him that she didn't like.

Without a thought, she wrapped her arms around him. The wet spots on his shirt touched her cheek, and she kissed him there.

"Heard that, did ya?"

She nodded against his chest, too afraid to talk as she might be the one crying against his chest this time.

"He's a good boy," Cage said and wrapped his arms around her. "I just couldn't let him think that this was only temporary."

"He was so happy," she said and looked up at him.

Cage nodded and looked away. She could see that she wasn't the only one who was emotional from it.

"You know, a boy like that could really use a dog," she said.

Cage looked back at her and frowned.

"What kind of dog?"

She smiled up at him. "The kind that a kid might risk his life saving."

Realization swept over his face. "Hank."

She nodded against him. "He loves that dog."

Cage smoothed a hand on her back. "I thought you loved Hank."

She smiled and kept her face hidden. There was no way she'd be able to get through this if she looked at him.

"I do," she said. "But I have a feeling there will be plenty of opportunities to see him."

She gasped as he pulled her back and hungrily pressed his mouth to hers. Whitney wrapped her hands around his neck and held on as he plundered her mouth.

When she finally pulled away, she was more than a little aroused and very winded.

"Every night," Cage said.

Her eyebrows shot up in shock. "I don't know if I can keep up with you."

Cage let out a bark of laughter. "No, you'll see Hank every night."

Whitney blushed but moved a little closer. "I will?"

"Yes," he said. "I can't stand not to see you. Life is short, and I intend to make the most of it."

She nibbled her lip. There were so many things she wanted to do right now, and a dinner party was about as far from those as she could get.

"Later," Cage growled as if he were reading her mind.

During one last sweet kiss, Whitney dangled herself from his arms and linked their hands together.

This was how it was supposed to be.

* * *

The ride home was far more somber than Cage anticipated. Despite working things out, reality had come crashing down on them when Reed told the family about the struggles Olivia had been having carrying their child.

It was just a stark reminder of how focused the family had been on Cage's recovery that no one seemed to see his brother's family's suffering.

This was only compounded by news about a serious illness affecting Sarah, the wife of his second to eldest brother, Jett. No one seemed to know what was wrong, but she'd had a fever for a week now and couldn't keep things down. All they could do was hope that the newest medicine she'd been given would do the trick.

"Do you think Reed's wife will be okay?" Whitney asked as they drove home.

Cage glanced in the mirror to make sure Alex was sleeping.

He sighed. "She's a fighter, but if Reed's worried, it means things are serious."

She reached over and took his hand. He liked that she wanted to comfort him.

"Listening to what the doctors say is the best bet she has," Whitney said. "We should make them something to eat, so she doesn't have to worry about it."

Cage glanced over at her and smiled. Every time he talked with her, his love grew.

"That would be nice," he said quietly. "Reed is going to be home more. With all the recent activity, the men have been working twice as much." He absently stroked her fingers. "We have to be more vigilant with work details."

Whitney squeezed his hand hard. "Is it really so dangerous?"

Cage sighed. He could lie. Everything in him said to, but if they were going to have anything, she had to know what life with him was like.

"Yes," he said finally. "I've seen the worst in the world, and sometimes people don't come back in this line of work. But I'm good at it. I get to protect the people I love, and that's important to me. Sometimes we make sacrifices to protect the people we love."

He looked over at her and squeezed her hand. Maybe it was the chicken shit way to tell her, but at least he had.

She squeezed his hand back and looked out the window.

When she spoke again, he could tell she was fighting back tears.

"You just make sure you are one of the ones that comes back," she said.

His heat thumped in his chest. Knowing she cared was enough for now, and he'd take whatever he could.

"I'll always come back," he whispered.

CHAPTER EIGHTEEN

"CAGE!"

Whitney's voice cut through his sleepy mind, and he opened his eyes.

"Wake up, Cage!" This time her panicked words pulled him wide awake.

Cage sat up quickly.

"What's going on?" he asked.

Whitney flipped on the light. Her face paled, and she paced around frantically.

"He's gone, Cage," she said and pulled out a note.

He hopped out of bed and took the paper.

A message had been scrawled in pencil:

Sometimes you have to protect the people you love,
Alex

"Shit," Cage said and raced over to the chair his pants were slung over.

This was his fault. Alex had misunderstood all that stuff he'd said. He wasn't talking about the kid protecting them. That was Cage's fucking job. All Alex needed to do was be a kid and grow up happy, maybe have a family and make his grandfather proud.

Cage tugged on the pants and ignored the pain that came from moving his leg without stretching his muscles.

"Cage," Whitney said.

Tears streamed down her face as she struggled to keep herself under control.

He hurried over to her and hugged her tightly.

"I'll get a hold of Trent. We'll find him," Cage whispered.

He gave her one last hug before standing and slipping on his shirt.

The more time he spent there, the less of a chance the kid had.

Cage dialed Trent, but his call went to voicemail.

"Call me," he said to the voicemail. "The kid's gone, and we could use your help."

He hung up and scanned over the numbers. Reed would normally be his first choice, but if Olivia heard what had happened, there was no telling how things would turn out.

Ryder. He was the most capable of handling this.

Cage touched the name on his phone's screen and waited.

"This better be important," Ryder mumbled into the phone.

"It is," Cage said. "Alex is gone, and I need your help."

"I'll be right over," Ryder said, sounding far more alert than Cage would have thought possible given the situation.

"Not here." He glanced over at the light from the bathroom where Whitney was dressing. He shut the door to the bedroom. "He went home," Cage said, pacing the floor. "They'll kill him if they find him."

"Damn."

"I'll meet you there." Cage pulled out his top drawer. "Oh, no," he said and riffled through the drawer, hoping that he might be wrong. "Oh, this is fucking bad."

"Cage?" Ryder said on the other end of the phone, his voice tight with worry.

"The kid's got one of my guns."

Whitney gasped at the doorway. A gun? What did a boy know about guns?

"Meet me there," Cage said quickly into the phone and hurried over to her. "I'm sure he's fine." He held her close. The warmth of his body wasn't enough to stop the ache that poured through her. "We'll find him."

She nodded against him and pushed him to the door. If Cage was going to find him, she had to let him go and be strong.

"What about the police?" she said.

"Have to time this right, or it's going to end badly for everyone. Let me handle all of that."

"Go," she said and started toward the front door. "I'll stay here in case he comes back."

Cage nodded and stepped onto the porch.

"Cage," she called. Her voice cracked as she called out to him. "You call as soon as you have him. You understand? As soon as you have him."

She watched as he nodded.

"Call my mother," he said and pointed to the back where his family's number was written on a paper for Alex. "She'll know what to do."

Whitney nodded and held back the tears. Hank whimpered beside her, and she knew he was worried as well.

She took in a deep breath and looked down at the sad little dog.

"No time for that," she said and took in a deep breath. "We've got calls to make."

* * *

Cage raced through the dark streets of the city until he approached the bike shop. He flicked off his lights and drove quietly along the streets near the building. The last thing he needed was to get spotted before he wanted them to see him. He wasn't sure this could end without someone getting shot, but he damned wanted to make sure it wasn't him or Alex.

He had no idea what the plan was besides seeing if Alex was there and beating the shit out of anyone that tried to stop him from getting that kid back.

His hands clenched the steering wheel.

Ryder was already across the street in a hidden grassy patch with his bike. Cage pulled in next to him and cut the engine.

He climbed out and stood next to his brother as they watched the place.

"You know this is fucking crazy," Ryder said.

Cage shrugged. "So says the man who charged up a mountain and fought off a biker gang."

Ryder turned and grinned at him. "So we're both fucking stupid. Pretty sure that's genetic."

Cage chuckled as he watched the building across the way. From their position, they were never going to see anything.

"I need to get closer," Cage said and started to walk forward. He stopped when Ryder placed a hand in front of him.

"With caution," Ryder said.

They hurried across the road and made their way to the front. When Ryder went to peer into the front window, Cage stopped him and pointed to the overhead cameras.

Ryder nodded, and they walked the opposite direction. Cage recognized the area. It was where he'd first met Carlos and Alex. At that time they'd been seeking information about a recent crime. Now they were there for a whole new reason. Crates lined the wall. He pointed toward them.

"I can't climb, but you can," he said.

Ryder crept his way up the crates and looked in the dirty window.

He held up five fingers. Five guys. They could handle five guys if they planned it right.

Ryder turned and stepped down from the crates as easily as he had climbed them.

"Kid's in there," he said. He frowned and looked away.

"Tell me," Cage said and clenched his fist. He could take it.

"They have him in a cage," Ryder said.

Cage opened his mouth to say something else but stopped as bright lights shot out from the other side of the building.

They ducked behind the crates and hoped no one came their direction.

A door creaked open on a truck, and someone heavy stepped out.

"Let's get this shit loaded," a man grunted. He spit loudly.

Cage strained to hear what was happening.

Another man laughed nasally. "Yeah, like you got somewhere to be."

The other man huffed and shifted his feet on the gravel.

"Fuck you," he grunted. "I've got a date."

The nasally man laughed. "With what? Your hand?"

"Listen here, you little puta." The other man crunched across the gravel.

"Knock it off, you dickheads," another man shouted.

Cage shifted where he stood. The weight of his body on his knee was killing him. Gravel stirred near him, and the voices stopped.

"What was that?" the nasally man asked.

A beam of light spread out along the side of the building. If they turned the corner, they'd have no choice but to fight. Cage pulled out his gun and waited.

The light landed on a stray cat, started by the intrusion of light.

"Little fucker," the driver grunted.

Two shots rang through the air at the cat. Cage watched as the cat fell to the ground.

Bile rose in his throat, but he fought the feeling.

"No!"

Cage tensed at the sound of Alex. The cage rattled as he shouted.

"You didn't have to," Alex said to the men. The leader was the first to speak.

"No," he said. "Tomas didn't have to shoot the cat, but

that's what happens when you cross the Los Malos."

The man spit, and Cage could only guess where it landed.

"Where's Roberto?" Alex said. "I want to see Roberto."

Tomas laughed. "He wants to see the boss. I say we load him up and take him there."

Cage shook his head and looked back to Ryder.

He held up his hand for Cage to stay in position.

Cage glared at him but kept still. Coming out now wasn't likely to help. Three against two with better cover, with additional reinforcements nearby, and the Los Malos had a hostage. At least this way, they knew Alex wouldn't be immediately killed.

"Load up," the leader said.

They listened as three sets of feet made their way to the truck. Ryder nodded to the road across the way. He wanted them to sprint across to the car before the men drove out.

Cage nodded.

With everything he had, Cage pushed his knee further. It shook with each impact, and he only hoped the damage he was doing wasn't permanent.

Sweat poured down his face.

He slipped into the brush as the truck made its way from behind the garage.

"Get ready to drive," Ryder said in his ear, sliding onto his bike.

Cage looked over to his brother. "Don't let that truck out of your sight."

Ryder nodded and started the engine once the truck had passed and tore off after them.

Cage jumped in his car and kept a hard eye on his brother as he tried to keep up.

No matter what happened, he was getting Alex the fuck out of there. And if he could take out a few of the bastards while he was at it, so be it.

CHAPTER NINETEEN

CAGE STEPPED OUT OF HIS CAR and watched as the truck backed up to a warehouse off the pier.

"We need a plan," Ryder said.

Cage stared at his elder brother for a moment before talking.

"I'm the bait," he said. "They'd love to finish me off, especially Roberto," he said. "You need to find a way to take out a bunch of them at once before they kill the both of us."

Ryder looked at him like he'd gone crazy. "Can we talk about a real plan? We need a plan that that doesn't get you shot."

Cage lifted a brow at the last statement.

Ryder sighed. "Again."

Cage looked over the building and shook his head. He really didn't see many other options. They didn't have the numbers the Los Malos now did, and even if they did, he doubted that his people would be able to get there in time.

No, it was just them, and they were going to have to make this work, or Alex would never make it out of there alive.

Cage made his way to the side of the building. He was slightly surprised to find that there weren't any men manning the door, but Carlos had said that the new crew didn't really have much experience under their belt.

He stopped at a trashcan and frowned. Cage lifted the lid. The stench that wafted through made him gag and nearly retch.

"What the hell is that?" Ryder asked from beside him and

covered his mouth.

Cage looked over the side into the bin. He turned away at the sight of a dead dog.

"What the fuck?" Ryder said, and Cage could only nod. Whatever the hell was going on, they were killing some dogs. Killing pets and planning to kill a kid. The Los Malos were certainly living up to their name.

Cage closed the lid and stepped away from the can. He had to clear his head.

"We need to get inside," he said and moved to the side door. "We're never going to know what's going on if we don't."

Ryder shook his head. "We don't know what's on the other side of that door. You could be walking into a firefight you can't get out of."

Cage clenched his fists. The more time they spent out in the alley, the slimmer Alex's chances became.

"I'm going—"

He stopped when the door creaked open a little.

"You get it," Tomas said on the other side of the door.

"Don't let it touch me," the nasally man said.

The Allens hurried to the other side of the trash as the men slowly made their way out.

They opened the first can, and the stench of rot filled the air.

"When are they going to pick up this thing?" Tomas grunted.

The sound of something hitting the pile struck fear into Cage. It could be Alex. Maybe they were already finished with him.

The nasally man slammed the lid back in place.

"They were supposed to be here today, but maybe boss got the day wrong," the nasally man said.

Tomas chuckled a little. "Don't let him hear you say that."

The nasally man grumbled as they made their way back

inside. When the door had clicked behind them, Cage stumbled out of his hiding spot.

"Let me look," Ryder said and placed a hand on his shoulder.

Cage shook his head. "I have to know."

He shook off the hand and moved slowly to the can. His hand shook as he lifted up and peeked inside. Another dead dog. He was both disgusted and relieved.

When he turned back to his brother, Ryder sighed and nodded.

"Fine," he said. "Stick to the edges of the building and try to find out what you can. If we can get the boy out before they notice, that would be our best shot."

Cage looked to the door and gritted his teeth.

He looked back to Ryder when he shook Cage's shoulders a little.

"Keep your head," Ryder said. "I'll meet you on the other side, and for God's sake, don't go looking for trouble."

Cage nodded.

He turned and crept to the door. If he could get in without being noticed, he might actually have a chance.

The handle squeaked as he turned it, but there was no going back now. If they heard the door, they would already be waiting for him. Cage took a breath and pulled open the door.

Nothing.

He looked back to Ryder and gave the all clear. His brother nodded and started toward the back of the building. All they had to do was find the kid. No big deal.

Cage crept along the wall like his brother suggested. He found that from there he could get a clear picture of what was going on.

Crates stuffed with dogs lay everywhere. On one wall, several lay quietly in their crates as he passed by. The lack of barking or whimpering unnerved him. None even bothered to wag their tails. After what he'd just seen, Cage wondered if they were even alive.

The next section explained the quiet state of the dogs. Cage peeked through several of the crates and watched in horror as a man in a white coat stuck a syringe into a dog's neck that had been strapped to the table.

The dog yelped once, but within seconds was lying quietly against the metal table. His tongue lolled out the side of his mouth. Without pausing, the man in the coat felt around the dog's fur. When he stopped, he reached over and grabbed the scalpel from the table. A quick cut to the back of the neck, and he was digging around under the skin. Within a few moments, the man pulled out something and tossed it onto the table.

He stapled the skin back together.

"Next," he shouted.

Two men sitting near him pulled the dog off the table and placed it back into the crate where it was moved near the wall with the other sedated dogs.

The man came back and sprayed off the table and tools with a hose.

Cage took deep breaths as he struggled to keep under control. Blowing his fuse here wasn't going to do anything for Alex.

He moved back to the wall and made his way closer to the front of the building. It was a little quieter there.

"Just like your grandfather," Roberto said from nearby. Cage ducked down under some large parts that hung from the ceiling.

Several Los Malos stood around Roberto. Some grinned at Alex. Others looked bored.

Cage nearly shouted when Alex came into sight. His face was bloodied, and he looked like he might have some black eyes, but he was alive.

A flash of metal gleamed from the back of his pants under his jacket. Apparently, the Los Malos hadn't thought of him as enough of a threat to search. In another situation, Cage would have been happy for their sloppiness, but not this time.

"No, no, no," Cage whispered to himself.

He could only hope that the kid had wised up and wouldn't be able to follow through with his plan.

"Don't you talk about abuelo," the boy said.

Roberto stepped a little closer and laughed.

"He wasn't so smart." Roberto grinned at Alex and kicked his cage. "Stepping in for the cojo."

Cage didn't know what they meant, but if he had to guess, it had something to do with him.

Alex placed his hand around his back.

Cage gritted his teeth. He was out of options. If he started a firefight so near Alex, the boy was likely to get shot.

"Hey," Cage said, sliding out from his spot. "Maybe you should pick on someone your own size."

He needed to buy time for Ryder. Either way, the boy would be safe for a bit longer.

Roberto's eyes widened in surprise.

Men raised and pointed their guns at Cage.

Cage tossed his gun to the ground. It clattered loudly and slid out of reach.

Roberto held up a hand as several men shouted to him in Spanish.

"Cage," Alex cried out.

Cage gave him a half-smile. "Hey," he said and eyed the men around the room as he spoke to Alex. "Fancy meeting you here."

Roberto rushed forward. His pony tail bounced on the back of his head as he moved.

"Looks like the cojo decided to save the day." Roberto stopped in front of him and gave him a wicked smile.

Two men came from behind Cage and grabbed his arms, holding them out to his side.

"So let me ask you, cojo," Roberto moved to the side of him. Just close enough to whisper. "How's the knee?"

Blinding pain shot through his leg as Roberto smashed his foot into it. Cage cried out, unable to stop himself.

When he was able to focus again, his eyes found Alex. His hands were around his back. Cage could only guess they were gripping the cold handle of the gun.

He shook his head a little.

This time the blow came to the side of his face.

Cage spit on the floor. Blood tinted the color. He turned back to Roberto and grinned.

"For a skinny little bastard, you can sure hit."

Roberto's mouth twisted to a dry smile.

"I'm glad you feel that way," he said and nodded to one of the men behind him. "Hold him down," he said and laughed. "I think we'll have a little fun." He nodded toward Alex. "A little something to look forward to."

The man behind him laughed and punched Cage hard on the side of the head. The world spun for a moment as he tumbled to the ground. More pain lanced through his leg as he landed on it. Another man kicked him hard. If that only gave him a broken rib or two, he'd be lucky.

Rough hands came on either side of his body and held his arms down.

He turned to look at Alex, who still had his hand behind his back. Cage struggled to shake his head at the kid.

"Family bonding moment?" Roberto said from near his feet.

The flash of the scalpel in his hand sparked fear. This man wasn't just a monster, but he was insane.

"Now how about some real fun?" Roberto laughed. His voice was high, and Cage swallowed hard.

He jumped when a shot rang out and took down the man holding his left arm. Another shot rang out from a different direction, taking out another man.

"Take cover," someone shouted.

Cage pulled away and pushed Alex's crate out of the line of fire. He leg throbbed like never before, and unlike the other time when he'd pushed it too far, there was no putting any weight on it. He crawled under the heavy machine part he'd been under before and pushed Alex back even further.

"Here," Alex said through the slats and shoved the gun through.

Cage took the piece. He checked the clip and then aimed at the Los Malos. There weren't many bullets in the gun, and he wasn't even sure he'd be able to hit much in his current state.

More shots rang out, and the Los Malos looked around, desperate to respond to their attackers.

Sirens sounded in the distance.

"Policia," someone shouted, and Cage let out a loud sigh.

He leaned hard against the crate containing Alex. The room faded in and out as he tried to take deep breaths. Each time he did, his battered ribs ached.

"Cage," Alex said near his head. His little hand came through the grate and touched his cheek.

"You weren't supposed to follow me," Alex said to Cage, tears streaming down his face.

Cage took a pained breath. "You are my family," he said and turned slightly to look at the boy. "I'm supposed to follow you." He smiled. "That's what we do."

"Clear!" Cage heard someone shout. It sounded like Trent, which confused Cage. He hadn't even been able to get a hold of the other man.

"Cage," Whitney's voice echoed off the walls. "Alex."

His eyes focused as she came running.

"No," he said quickly and tried to move but fell limp on the floor. "It's too dangerous."

He stopped and listened. There was no gunfire. The pain clouded his mind, and he tried to figure out why Trent, let alone Whitney, were at the warehouse.

Whitney knelt next to the cage and picked up the gun he'd dropped to the floor.

With two hard hits to the lock, it popped open.

She pulled out the boy and hugged him tightly. Cage pushed himself up to sitting and hissed as his leg moved with him.

Moments later, he was being hugged tightly. Whitney hadn't released Alex and held them both tightly.

"Neither of you do that to me again." She shook as she spoke. "I was so scared. I thought I'd lost you both, and it was like feeling my heart being ripped to a million pieces."

"I'm sorry," Alex cried against her.

She hugged him even tighter. Cage strained to wrap his arms around them both but found the ability somehow.

"Never again," she said and looked over to Cage. "You will never again pull that sort of stunt. For as long as either of you live."

"Understood," he said, closing his eyes again.

* * *

Whitney sat next to Cage in the hospital. It was the first bit of quiet she'd had in the last twenty-four hours, and despite how things had gone, she knew she was lucky to even be sitting here with him. They had been so close to losing the two of them forever.

If Trent hadn't arrived in time or Ryder had failed to take out the men at the back of the building, Cage and Alex would be gone.

His hand twitched in hers, and she rubbed her thumb over it. He would live. She glanced to his leg and swallowed.

"Hey," Cage said and pulled her from the dark thoughts.

She smiled at him. "Hey," she said.

He grimaced as he tried to sit up, and she placed a hand

on his chest.

"Be careful."

He lay back against the bed but sat back up in a panic.

"Alex," he said.

She pushed a little harder on his chest.

"He's with your parents," she said and was glad when he relaxed under her hand.

"Thank God," he whispered and closed his eyes.

She watched as her hand on his chest rose and fell. He was still for so long, she started to pull back.

"Stay," he whispered. His eyes opened and focused on her.

Even like this, he still took her breath away.

"What happened?" he asked. "How did you know we were there?"

"I came with the police."

"How did you get the police there so fast?"

Whitney opened her mouth but stopped when Trent came in.

"I'm afraid that's me," he said and took a seat next to Whitney.

Cage frowned. He knew he must be on something, but the situation was just beyond strange.

"You?" he said.

Trent cleared his throat. "I got a lead," he said and leaned forward. "Actually, my dad did via some of his police contacts. None of the guys seemed interested, so I decided to check it out myself."

Cage narrowed his eyes at him.

"And you did this by yourself?" Cage asked.

Trent nodded. "Look," he said and sighed. "We were looking for evidence, and that's just what I was going for. Snap a few pic, and it would be perfect. That way we could be the heroes without busting in guns blazing."

Cage grunted. Sounded a bit too much like Ryder.

"What was the tip?" Whitney asked.

Trent looked to Cage. "Sanitation complained about the dumpster. Said it smelled worse than the packing plants."

Whitney turned white, and he knew she was piecing things together.

"Kace worked out the rest and rallied the cops to come to our rescue," Trent said with a grin. "Or maybe my dad and your brother threatened the hell out of them."

Cage nodded and grinned back. It sounded exactly like those two. The smile faded as Roberto's face flashed in his head.

"And Roberto?"

Trent shook his head. "They were able to make a number of arrests, but Roberto was nowhere to be found."

Cage shook his head. That man was beyond dangerous.

"Why were they even doing it?"

"They had a couple of big buyers interested in a lot of untraceable animals. The Los Malos thought it'd just be a good way to make cash without attracting the same level of attention that drugs or guns might. Hell, it worked, given how little attention the police were paying to them."

"Why couldn't we see any activity?"

"They'd been moving around every night. Some of it had to do with a contact they had in the Sanitation Department. Looks like their guy had been getting sloppy helping them clean up though."

"I think he needs to rest," Whitney said when Cage closed his eyes for a moment. The door clicked shut a few moments later.

"I'm fine," he mumbled.

He smiled when she kissed him softly on the lips. "That's the morphine talking," she whispered. "Go to sleep."

His heart swelled as he reached out to take her hand in his. She laced their fingers together.

His breathing fell into a steady pattern. He listened to the quiet sounds of the room and let the world around him drift in and out. Whitney leaned forward kissed his hand, and he could almost see her in his head.

"My love," she whispered.

The world faded around him as he drifted into a blissful slumber.

CHAPTER TWENTY

CAGE HATED THE GOWNS they made him wear every time he went to see the damn doctor. After so many years, he would have thought they'd come up with something better than a gown that showed off his ass. At least he got to keep his underwear.

A quick rap came at the door, and an older man in a white coat entered.

"Hi, Cage," the doctor said and stuck out his hand. "Doctor Field said you've made amazing progress these last few weeks."

Cage grunted. Progress was what they kept calling it, but it still wasn't much.

"You're able to stand without much pain and even have decent function." The man smiled. Cage glared at his name tag. Doug Douglas. What the hell kind of name was that for a non-cartoon doctor?

The man reached out and placed a hand on his shoulder. "Look, son," he said. "I know you don't think that it's much, but you are doing so well."

Cage frowned. He didn't need a damn pep talk. What he needed was for someone to actually fix his damn knee.

"You are lucky to be able to walk," he continued.

Cage rolled his eyes and sighed loudly.

"When will I be able to do more?" he asked.

The smiled faded from the man's face a little. "I thought someone had told you," he said. "I just assumed."

Cage waited as he let loose.

"The chances of you ever getting full function back are nearly non-existent. The recent incident resulted in a lot of severe damage."

His mind shut off as the doctor continued to talk about his limited function and what that meant.

Most of the speech was the same thing over and over. Don't push, don't try, just accept it.

Cage clenched his fists until the man left the room, and he was able to put on his normal clothes.

He had to get out of there. As quickly as he could, Cage made his way out of the building and back to his car.

His new SUV roared to life, and although it had nothing on his sports car, it did just fine cutting out of the parking lot.

As he made his way home, Cage thought about how many times he'd been told no over the last few weeks. It was like the world wanted to see him limping. Maybe Roberto was right, and he was just a lame cripple.

Cage stopped hard outside the house. He tromped up to the front door, and when he opened the door, he found Trent and Alex playing a game of cards.

"Hey," Trent said and looked up at Cage. "How was the... Hey, Alex. Let's go to the park and maybe get ice cream."

Cage nodded to him as Trent gathered up Hank and the boy.

Right now he had only one thing on his mind.

* * *

Whitney hummed in the shower. The warm stream was like her own personal massage. She groaned under the spray.

Warm finger trailed down her back, and she gasped at the feeling. She knew those hands better than she knew her own.

Cage pressed flush against her back, and she leaned back into him.

"I didn't know you were home," she said and looked at him over her shoulder. "How did things go with the doc—"

Cage sealed his mouth over hers, silencing her.

She groaned and rubbed herself against him. His thick, hard cock slid between her legs and against her wet center.

Whitney moaned against his mouth.

Cage pulled back and trailed wet kisses along her neck, sucking the tender parts that made her squirm with need.

His fingers traced the path along her sides and around to her stomach, stopping just under the swell of her breasts.

Slowly, he traced his fingers all along the breasts, never touching her hardened peaks.

She moaned loudly as he sped up the movement behind her and tried to muffle the sound against her arm.

"They went out," he said roughly in her ear. His licked the lobe, and she shivered.

Whitney was tired of the teasing. It was her turn. She reached between her legs and rubbed her hands along his hot shaft, letting the head slip between her fingers, so it would press hard against her clit.

"Fuck, baby," Cage groaned. His hips pulled back, and she huffed.

"That's no fair," she said and opened her mouth to say something else when he pinched her nipples.

Whitney shivered in his arms as her insides quivered with need.

She could feel him pressed against her opening, the head slipping in slightly and teasing her as to what would come.

"Cage," she moaned. "Please."

As the words left her lips, Cage pressed himself deep inside her with one push.

She shivered around him and could feel her juices run down her thighs. When she returned her hand back between her legs, Whitney could feel him stretching her wide.

He pressed her against the wall, the cold tile a stark contrast against her hot, hard nipples.

Cage gripped her hips with a force she'd never seen and slammed hard into her.

She moaned loudly at the strength he used and rubbed herself.

"You're so wet for me," he whispered in her ear.

It made her feel naughty, and Whitney increased the pressure on her clit.

"Only for you," she said, her words like a breath.

Cage hammered into her now, slapping against her wet pussy so hard that she wondered if either of them would be able to stand after this.

He leaned over her and pushed deep inside, rotating his hips in small circles as she clutched to the wall for dear life.

"More," she moaned and pressed hard against him. His hands squeezed hard on her hips.

He sped up, each time pressing more into her then he had before.

With one final thrust, she came hard around him, her pussy milking every last drop out of his cock.

After a moment, she tilted her hips forward and turned in his arms.

"Rough day?" she said and kissed him softly on the mouth.

Cage grinned against her mouth.

"Not anymore," he said and rested his head on her shoulder.

She kissed the side of his face and enjoyed the closeness. He had been suffering since the hospital, and there wasn't much she could do about it.

"I'll never have full function," he said.

Whitney stroked a hand through his hair.

"Well, that sort of seemed like fun function to me." She grinned at him.

Cage laughed. "I think that's always going to work out fine," he said.

Whitney wrapped her arms around him.

"You will just have to settle for being as you are," she said.

He grew quiet, and she knew he was thinking about that.

"And what about you?" he asked and leaned back.

Whitney shook a little as she stared at him. This was a real question from the real man.

"I will always love you just as you are," she said and kept her eyes on him.

A smile spread across his face as she continued to stare.

"I wondered when you were going to say it again." He grinned back at her. "Waiting until a man's unconscious isn't really a fair fight."

Heat flamed her face as she struggled to step out of the shower.

"Wait," he said, and she looked back at him.

"So you can tease me?" she asked.

Cage shook his head and pressed a gentle kiss against her mouth.

"I love you too," he whispered.

Tears ran down her face as she took in his words.

She wrapped her arms around him and kissed him hard on the mouth. Her tongue swiped the seam.

Cage pulled back to stare at her. "If you don't stop, I'm going to have to show you how much I love you."

Whitney chewed on her lip and smiled at him.

"I think I'm going to need a demonstration." She giggled.

Cage growled and turned her in his arms and pressed her against his growing length.

"I will show every day for the rest of my life," he whispered in her ear and she shivered against him.

"I look forward to it."

A Note from Madison

Thank you for reading *Cage*. If you enjoyed this book, please consider reviewing it. We authors live and die by reviews.

Please keep an eye out for my next romantic suspense book, *Noel*.

You can join my release mailing list at
http://eepurl.com/OX9r5

ALSO BY MADISON STEVENS

Allen Securities (Romantic Suspense)

Reed (Allen Securities #1)
Kace (Allen Securities #2)
Liam (Allen Securities #3)
Ryder (Allen Securities #4)

Kelly Clan (Romantic Suspense)

Finn (Kelly Clan #1)
Conor (Kelly Clan #2)
Noel (Kelly Clan #3)

Luna Lodge (Paranormal Romance)

Sol (Luna Lodge #1)
Titus (Luna Lodge #2)
Lucius (Luna Lodge #3)
Marius (Luna Lodge #4)
Apollo (Luna Lodge #5)
Apollo and Val (Luna Lodge #5.5)
Remus (Luna Lodge #6)
Justus (Luna Lodge #7)

Shadow Series

Shadow's Embrace (Shadow #1)

Special Forces

Trent (Special Forces #1)

Road House (Contemporary Romance Short Stories)

Letting Go (Road House #1)
Holding On (Road House #2)
Standing By (Road House #3)

Privileged (New Adult Romance)

Privileged (Privileged #1)
Elite (Privileged #2)

Author Bio

Madison currently lives with her husband and two children in the Valley of the Sun in Arizona. After leaving the frozen tundra of the north, she was more surprised than anyone with how much she has enjoyed living in the desert. Seeing as she stated on more than one occasion before moving to Arizona how much she hated heat, it was an odd move, but it seems her hatred for sub-zero temperatures and ice has won out in the end.

When she's not writing, she's enjoying time with her family. Madison and her family frequent festivals in the area, as well as local cultural events, and spend time with family in the area. In the summer, she is most likely to be found in the pool with the family and in the winter by the fireplace. Since both her children are autistic, days can be a little chaotic, but with her husband beside her, there's nothing she can't handle.

Madison's blog is located at
http://madisonstevensauthor.com/

She can be contacted at madisonstevensauthor@gmail.com

Printed in Great Britain
by Amazon

82294275R00099